April 20, 07

WILFRED

The Devil's Disciple

To Judy & Butch, my very good friends This book could have easily been titled "NORMAN The Devils Disciple" ed

Edward T. Duranty

Edward T. Duranty

Bloomington, IN Milton Keynes, UK

authorHOUSE®

AuthorHouse™
1663 Liberty Drive,
Suite 200
Bloomington, IN 47403
www.authorhouse.com
Phone: 1-800-839-8640

AuthorHouse™ UK Ltd.
500 Avebury Boulevard
Central Milton Keynes,
MK9 2BE
www.authorhouse.co.uk
Phone: 08001974150

First published by AuthorHouse   3/14/2007

ISBN: 978-1-4259-9691-8 (sc)

Library of Congress Control Number: 2007901286

Printed in the United States of America
Bloomington, Indiana

This book is printed on acid-free paper.

Dedicated to Elaine,
my wife of forty six years.

Prologue

Wilfred Magnum would never know who his parents were or exactly when or where he was born. His date of birth registered with the Town Clerks Office was May 4, 1939. The date coincided with the day he was abandoned on the front door steps of St. Matthew's Convent in Whitefield, Minnesota.

From The Author

The moment in time sequences and the chronological order of historical development concerning the narrative substance of the story line, were intentionally distorted for the purpose of creating fictional characters in a fictitious novel. The character names are imaginary: any resemblance to real life individuals is purely coincidental.

Introduction

*H*ave you ever wondered if evil spirits, the disciples of the devil, really exist? No? Then why are most of us afraid to walk through a graveyard alone on a dark, gloomy night? Is it because we are afraid of the unknown?

Various passages from old scripture describe how Satan could adopt a spirit form, reside within a person, and influence his or her thoughts and behavior.

The authors of these chronicles had good reason to believe that evil spirits exist. They saw their manifestations with their own eyes or they heard the testimonies of witnesses whom they knew and trusted. They recognized demonic possession as a weapon of Satan, employed for the sole purpose of undermining everything good, creating evil, and paying homage to the Angel of Darkness.

Wilfred Magnum is a story of a baby who at birth was possessed by Satan and instilled with demonic powers of evil. The off spring of a shantytown whore and fathered by a half breed albino Indian; he was easy prey for the wiles of the devil. Born in an environment where human emotions were nonexistent his mission was the perpetration of evil. As a child of the devil he could use his powers to inflict, suffering, pain and even death on those he perceived to be a threat to him.

Although vulnerable, when directly confronted he had the power to manipulate and control the movements of those who put him in jeopardy.

He had no conscience, pride, love or compassion.

He was evil incarnate, the ordained emissary of the Devil himself.

He would encounter a worthy foe, Father John Tobin. The battle waged would be good against evil. Who would be the victor?

Chapter 1

The doorbell sounded just as Sister Agnes was passing by the front entrance of the convent. Needing only a few seconds to answer the door, she startled a young woman who had placed a wicker basket on the front stoop. Immediately aware of the basket's content's, Sister Agnes tried to get her attention.

"Please come in, let me help you!"

The abruptness of the door opening and the nun's unexpected voice caught the woman by surprise. Her head bent to the ground, she hurriedly retreated back down the walkway, paying little heed to the Sisters pleas.

"Please! Please! Don't go! Let me help." It was to no avail; Sister Agnes raised her voice to a shout. "Stop! Please stop!"

Faltering for a moment, the woman paused, turned, and glared fiercely at the nun. Horrified, Sister Agnes clasped both hands to her face.

Trembling, she made the sign of the cross, her quivering voice barely audible.

"In the name of the Father, the Son, and the Holy Ghost."

Clutching her rosary beads, she stepped backwards, seeking the security of the convents doorway. Unable to bring herself to look away, Sister Agnes stood as though in a trance, staring at the appalling sight in front of her.

The woman's face was encased with multiple abscess sores. Scabs hung like feeding leeches from the bridge of her nose, extending downward to the underneath surface of her chin. Deteriorated white blood cells encircled the open sores with rings of white pus. These pustule mounds stretched her facial skin so taunt it forced her eye sockets to protrude outward, similar to the grotesque face of a sneering gargoyle.

In sheer disbelief, Sister Agnes watched as the girl opened the car door and slid across the front seat. The driver, partially concealed by the upper arc of the steering wheel, leaned sideways to assist her. The movement afforded Sister Agnes a clear view of a man's head. It appeared that a massive sore had solidified, encrusting most of his hairless scalp. As the man sat back up, she caught a brief glimpse of his face. There was no skin; exposed layers of fat tissue and bare bones were all that remained of his previous facial features.

The car engine roared as the vehicle began to accelerate and move forward. Passing the convent the car window lowered. Through rotted teeth and swollen lips, the woman screamed hysterically at the nun.

"He's evil! He's evil! He did this to us! He's the bastard son of the Devil."

Sister Agnes stood speechless as she tried to come to terms with what she had just witnessed. It would be hopeless to try to relate a true description of the couple's facial mutations to anyone, much less try to report it to the Mother Superior in St. Paul.

Jolted from her thoughts by the sudden sound of an infant's giggle, Sister Agnes retrieved the wicker basket and hastily retreated into the sanctity of the convent. As the door closed behind her, the sounds from the basket suddenly ceased!

Chapter 2

Their names were Todd and Janice Ingram. Until a short time ago, they had been the owners of a small trading post on the southern tip of Lake Red. As a child, Janice had nearly died from a severe bout of scarlet fever. The disease had left her with internal damage resulting in her inability to conceive. Their only avenue for acquiring a child was through the long process of adoption. As they continued to mull over the idea, a turn of events played into their hands.

A fur trapper who was friendly with the Ingram's had hurried to the trading post with news of a newborn baby for sale. The mother was a whore in one of the most evil and immoral shantytowns on the lakes. The baby was a boy and the price was three dollars.

At the same time the trapper was saying his goodbyes, a unit of cavalry soldier's on a routine patrol, had stopped at the lakes edge to water their horses. To the Ingram's it was a sign of spiritual intervention. How else could the trapper's news and the arrival of the soldiers be so precise? Running to the lake, Janice and Todd Ingram pleaded with the patrol sergeant for his help. Sympathetic to their plight, the sergeant agreed to escort them into the shantytown. He and his troopers would search for the newborn then escort them back to the trading post.

Todd mentioned that he had a car if that would help. Laughing the sergeant grinned at Todd.

"Not likely lad, not likely. The shantytown is located in a wilderness area on the western side of the lake. The only way to get there is by horseback."

The sergeant gave orders to saddle up two of the packhorses for the Ingram's to ride. They would leave their supplies at the trading post until they returned. Janice and Todd hurriedly prepared to leave. The trip would take them halfway around the lake.

Using old Indian trails and the lakes shoreline to guide by, the troop eventually found their way to the outer limits of the shantytown. Issuing a word of caution, the sergeant slowly led the patrol into the center of the town. The Ingram's gazed in disbelief at the shacks and the whores prancing about trying to get the attention of the troopers. They could only depict the shantytown as a second Sodom and Gomorrah.

It did not take long for the soldiers to find the whore with the baby for sale. Already back in business, she was entertaining two loggers in a small tin covered shack. Sitting upright on his mount, the sergeant called out for the woman to bring the infant outside. The whore came out carrying the infant in one hand, wrapped in a filthy rag. When she pinched its stomach, the baby cried out in pain. It was her way of proving that it was still alive. Laughing, she propped the baby up with both hands.

"This baby is very special."

The sergeant was amused.

"What was he, a virgin birth? Is that a couple of the Wise Men in your shack?"

The Sergeant's voice became tense.

"Tell me whore, just why is this baby so special? It could be real sad state of affairs, if I thought you were wasting my time!"

Holding the baby closer to her, she talked directly to the Ingram's. "One day I was at the edge of the lake washing myself when this albino Indian comes out of the woods, drags me out of the water, then takes me right there on the ground. Finishing himself off he starts pounding on his chest and a whooping it up. A few minutes later he up's and runs back into the woods. Never seen him again but I'll tell you that white Injun was hung like a horse."

The Sergeant was not impressed; Turning he gave his troops a harsh look, their laughter quickly ended.

"So what's your point, Whore? These people are here to buy the baby, so get on with it."

"The point, General, is that they tell me the white freak had the power to do strange things. The Indians speak of him as though he's some kind of a supernatural spirit. This baby is his son, so I figure that raises the price to at least five dollars."

The Ingram's were paying little heed to her story, their eyes were riveted on the poor little soul she held in her hands.

"I got two horny men waiting on me, the price is five dollars or like the last little bastard I had, I'll just feed him to the dogs."

Todd Ingram quickly nodded his head in agreement. The sergeant gave the whore her five dollars and then handed the baby over to Mrs. Ingram.

Wrapping the baby in a clean towel, Janice attempted to feed the baby using a nipple bottle containing goat's milk. If the baby was to survive it had to accept nourishment. Much to her relief the infant hungrily accepted the milk.

Forming up the unit to begin the return trip, the sergeant called his corporal to the forward position. The sergeant was still fuming over being given an ultimatum by a low life whore. He gave the corporal orders to take four men, return to the whores shack and retrieve the Ingram's five dollars.

"I want you to convey to her that I'm not a general! Trample her belongings, pull the shack down, and then catch up with us. Oh, I almost forgot, make sure she experiences the pain of having her stomach pinched."

Nodding his head in understanding the corporal turned his mount and went to the rear of the column. He was going to enjoy this.

A month had passed with the baby doing surprisingly well. The infant thrived on Janice's formula using goat's milk. The elated Ingram's had no problem passing the baby off as their newly adopted son.

Early one morning, a small band of Indians on horseback, dragging a makeshift litter, made its way to the front of the trading post. Todd went outside alone while Janice, armed with a scattergun, stood behind the curtains watching through the window. Fearing they might be hostile, Todd asked what they wanted. The Brave leading the column rode forward, stopping directly in front of him. Using sign language and speaking in broken English, the young Brave communicated that they meant no harm. Pointing toward the litter he spoke that the old one was a very powerful medicine man.

Sliding down from his horse, he motioned that Todd should follow him. Pausing for a moment he called out for Janice to join them. As they approached the litter they could see that the medicine man was very old. Wrapped only in a blanket he raised his hand in a gesture of welcome. The Ingram's bowed in recognition of his status. Pleased with their sign of respect, he addressed them in his native Indian tongue. The Brave did his best to make the Ingram's understand.

"The demon spirit that lived within the soul of the white Indian used the women to reach into the soul of your baby. The spirit is evil and will cause much harm. Take the baby to the center of the lake, weight him with stone, and cast him into the waters. If you do not destroy him he will destroy you. I can speak no more."

The medicine man raised his hand, closed his eyes and went to sleep.

The Brave walked the Ingram's back to the post.

"We are far from the reservation. The pony soldiers will soon be looking for us. We must leave now to seek the shelter of the forest. The medicine man traveled here to warn you, the white brave was his son! The Chief had the squaws stone him, until he could breath no more."

Mounting his horse the brave rode along side of the medicine mans litter. Giving the sign to leave, the Indians prodded their horses and began their return trip to the reservation.

The Ingram's stood watching until the Indians disappeared from view. Both were silent and deeply engrossed in their own thoughts. They had lived in the territory long enough to know that the appearance of a medicine man outside his tribal circle had to be extremely rare. To speak to white people was unheard of.

Taking his wife's hand, Todd suggested that they go inside, check on their son, and then discuss the Indian's words over a cup of hot tea. The baby was in a sound sleep. Janice and Todd had not yet agreed on a Christian name for their son. They had given themselves one more week to come to an agreement. If they could not, then all the selected names would be placed in a hat and the one drawn would become his given name.

Sitting across the table from one another, they sipped on their tea and waited for the other to speak. Janice was the first.

"He is so precious. I couldn't bear to give him up on the word of some old Indian. What if he was wrong and it was found out. We could be arrested for murder."

Todd reached over and took his wife's hand and held it gently.

"Janice, a medicine man is endowed with knowledge acquired by seers throughout the centuries. They speak only with wisdom and only for the betterment of the tribe. For a medicine man to travel for days on a litter, to inform a white man of impending disaster is beyond reality. I take his warning very seriously."

Just then a loud cry came from the baby's bed. Janice stood up in such a rush that she knocked over her chair. Going to the side of the infant's bed she looked down. He was grinning at her; his pretty blue eyes wide open. Covering him with a blanket, she placed her hand on his forehead. A few minutes later, he fell back asleep. Returning to the kitchen she was met by Todd's inquisitive look.

"Must of have had a little gas on his stomach. He fell right back to sleep."

Todd motioned for her to sit back down.

"I'll tell you what, we will keep a close watch on the baby. If anything what so ever happens out of the ordinary, I'll bring him back to the shantytown and leave him. Drowning we will not do, Okay?"

Not wanting to start an argument, Janice agreed. Again, a loud cry came from the bedroom.

That night, Janice did not sleep well she knew that she should of stuck up for the baby and not gave in to her husband's suggestion. Rising earlier than usual she went to the kitchen to wash. It was then that she noticed the small red welts streaking across the palm of her hand. Pausing for a moment, she thought back on what she could have touched!

As the day progressed, her hand became puffy and swollen. She showed her hands to Todd, asking him to drive her to Camp Ripley to see the doctor. "Maybe we can get the baby examined at the same time."

Todd looked at his wife's hands and agreed immediately.

"You know if we got a move on, we could have the camp chaplain baptize the baby. As a child of

God it would be protected from the Indian's evil spirit!

Janice took her husbands hand, she was so thankful for his kindness and love. Looking at his wife's face, he noticed a small growth on the bridge of her nose and a small reddish lesion on her left cheek. Rather than bring it to her attention, he would wait until they saw the military doctor.

"We will use our medicine man to fight the evil spirits."

Both were laughing as they rushed to get ready. Only a few minutes had passed when Todd noticed the red welts on his hands. For no apparent reason, the baby began to scream. Try as they might they could not get him to stop. The shill screaming was so intense that it pushed Janice towards near panic.

Todd yelled for her to calm down and go outside and get in the car. Instead she flew into a rage blaming him for the baby being upset.

"Maybe he could understand when you talked about bringing him back to that shantytown!"

Todd looked at his wife in disbelief, not for what she had just said but the appearance of her face. The tiny sore on her nose had grown larger and was spreading. The lesion on her cheek had also increased in size and appeared to be splitting into four separate sores. Looking down at the floor, he noticed a small clump of hair that had fallen from the back of his head. Giving himself a quick once over, he saw that the welts on his hands had become infected. His ears felt like they had been frost bitten. He became visibly upset when he found that he could easily pull out clumps of his own hair. Lost for words, he handed the mirror to his wife.

"Go ahead take a look."

Gasping she studied her face.

"Oh my God! What is happening to me?"

All at once, the baby stopped screaming and fussing. Todd and Janice quickly went to his bedside, the baby lay staring up at the two of them with a big grin on his face.

Todd had a 1940 Ford Sedan that he quickly loaded with blankets, pillows, some food items, and water. Ready to leave, he went back into the kitchen. His wife stood by helplessly as he took a small blanket and tucked the baby into a wicker basket. He couldn't believe the changes that had occurred on his wife's face in just the past half hour. The pain in his ears was increasing and both had turned black. A yellowish fluid was seeping slowly from each ear. Making contact with the air, it became sticky and adhered to the sides of his neck. Feeling the top of his head he couldn't believe that his hair was nearly gone.

"Hurry Janice, take the baby and get in the car we got to go for help!"

As Todd drove the state road to Camp Ripley, he knew that they were never going to return to the lake. His wife was a mass of sores, many which had abscessed and were infected. The medicine man had been right! The baby was destroying them. Janice hysterical began to cry uncontrollably.

"Oh Todd I am so very sorry."

There was nothing he could say. They were on the outskirts of Whitefield when it became obvious to Todd that a doctor would not do them any good.

"Janice, I am going to need your help. In a few minutes, I will tell you what you have to do. You must obey my order immediately, without question and not one second of delay. Can you do it?"

An unrecognizable Janice Ingram nodded painfully in agreement

Todd peered into the wicker basket, the baby seemed delightfully happy. Suddenly, he pulled the car up to the curb and stopped. He yelled at Janice!

"Now! Now! Open the door! Take the basket and run to the convent, leave it on the steps."

She barely left the car when the sound coming from the basket became more like a growl. Todd watched as Janice left the basket on the step and started back to the car. For a moment, it looked like a Nun was going to interfere. Janice stopped, looked back, and then hurried to the car. If nothing else he had tricked the little devil bastard. With the baby now under the control of the nuns he would have plenty of time to reach the river.

The Big Pine's violent rapids flowed undisturbed for over fifty miles. When and if they were ever found, all that would be left would be a few bleached bones.

Chapter 3

During the late eighteen hundreds, Scandinavian farmers immigrating from Denmark and Sweden settled predominately in the central region of Minnesota. The soil surrounding the areas of the Pequot Lakes contained layer upon layer of rich dark earth thanks to the geological movement of the ice age. For the immigrant farmer it was a virtual Shangri-la. The topography of the land was interspersed with numerous streams and lakes. Vast woodlands of Elm, Maple, Oak and White Pine provided the settlers with an unlimited supply of lumber for building farmhouses, outbuildings and fencing.

It also brought unscrupulous timber men who erected sawmills along side pristine waterways, without any thought to pollution. Loggers ravished the virgin forest leaving wide swaths of desolation behind them. Wild animals were virtually slaughtered by skinners and trappers for their hides and furs.

Unfortunately, along with the immigrant farmers came a multitude of malcontents looking for an easy way to make their fortunes or to steal somebody else's.

Shantytowns sprang up near to logging camps and Indian reservations. Incorrigible criminals, professional gamblers and con men abounded, always looking for a chance to separate a man from his money. Workers from the logging camps were their favorite targets. Using makeshift shacks, they would entice the loggers inside to gamble, drink liquor and be entertained by a bunch of thieving whores. The same tactic was used to lure the Indians off the reservations to rob them of their pelts and furs. Cavalry troops, ordered to restrict the Indians to their reservations, could often be bribed for a free night's stay with a shantytown lady.

Prostitutes inundated the shantytowns, spreading disease and finding themselves victims of unwanted pregnancies. No one knows how many fetuses and term infants were yanked from the comfort of the womb, only to gasp a few breaths of air, before entering the eternal darkness of death. Most, but not all shantytown whores were without conscience. Those still having a thread of decency would try to make arrangements to have their newborns taken to near by settlement and left there. If they were lucky they lived.

Construction workers imported from Duluth completed St. Matthew's Orphanage in early 1938. The Benedictine Sisters, the largest community of Catholic nuns in the world, financed the project. The management mission was to catholicize the settlers of the region as well as the White Earth Indian reservation to the west, the Leech Lake Indian reservation to the north and the Fond Du Lac Indian reservation to the east. The plan never materialized. The Indians, cheated out of their land, restricted to their reservations and living in squalor weren't in the greatest frame of mind to embrace the white man's god. Maybe his whisky, but not his god.

The sisters, while never questioning their Mother Superior's choice, were perplexed to why she had chosen Whitefield to build the convent. The population of Whitefield and its surrounding areas for the most part was ninety-nine percent Lutheran. Although cordial, the Lutherans would not accept the nuns into their domain. In 1521, the Pope had excommunicated their leader, Martin Luther, from the Catholic Church for disputing his Papacy. Four hundred and twenty years later, Luther's dogma that the scriptures were the sole authority for religious truths and not the Vatican's "ecclesiastical council," remained stronger than ever.

In the end, the convents staff of sixteen nuns was reduced to three, Sister Agnes, Sister Irene, and Sister Sylvia, who was elderly, incapacitated, and bed ridden. The convent sat on four acres of land on the northern edge of town. It was far enough from the center of town to afford the sisters a setting for spiritual privacy. Their day started at 6:00am, ending after evening prayers at 10:00pm. Once a month, a priest from Duluth would arrive bringing supplies, religious material, and mail that they did not want the local post office employees reading. The priest would say Mass for the two Sisters, and then leave to drive back to Duluth. Not once had a priest asked or inquired as to the well being of the bed ridden, Sister Sylvia.

Chapter 4

Sister Agnes, with the wicker basket in hand, hurried across the convent's large visitors' room to the infirmary. Regaining her composure, she met Sister Irene at the infirmary doorway.

"Draw a basin of warm water and bring it to the exam table, I'll need your help to remove the baby from the basket."

Sister Irene obeyed immediately. Time was a crucial element in the survival rate of an abandoned infant. Both Sister Agnes and Sister Irene had received extensive medical training as part of their commitment to the sisterhood. They were well aware that the infant's life could lie in their hands.

A few weeks earlier, an infant had been brought to the convent from a nearby shantytown. Feverish and comatose, the newborn was no more than two or three days old. The umbilical cord, still intact, was badly infected. The sisters, working in unison, tried in vain to sustain the life of this most precious being. Sister Irene performed the Sacrament of Baptism as the infant succumbed to its death. They knelt in prayer asking the Lord to receive the soul of this beautiful infant into His kingdom.

It was always a very trying time for both sisters. The town constable would be notified of the circumstances and time of death. He would then remand the remains to their care. Sister Irene would wrap the infant body in a white cloth and place it in a tiny wooden coffin.

The castaway baby would be laid to rest in a wooded cemetery in the back of the convent. Sister Irene would craft a small white wooden cross to adorn and mark the grave. Inscribed would be the date of death and the notation indicating a baby boy or baby girl. She would hand paint a small child like angel on both sides of the cross. In the cemetery there were angels painted on fourteen little white crosses.

When Sister Agnes had crossed the visitors floor of the convent it was her habit to glance up the stairway to the second floor. The room at the top of the landing belonged to Sister Sylvia. For just a split second Sister Agnes thought she saw the door move. She shrugged off the notion as "impossible," Sister Sylvia had been bed ridden for well over a year!

Sister Irene had readied a pan of tepid water, clean cloths and a small blanket on the examination table. The room had the resemblance of a typical hospital treatment room. A stainless steel table and an overhead lights made up the center of the room. A porcelain sink and a partially enclosed water closet took up one side of the room while a metal storage cabinet, containing medicines and medical equipment, filled in the corner. Three wide shelves lined the remaining back wall, decked out with neatly stacked piles of various bandages; washcloths, towels, diapers and other needed linens. The room was always ready for any type emergency.

Without a Doctor, many of Whitefield's Lutherans had no choice but to seek medical treatment at the convent.

Placing the basket on the exam table the Sisters prepared themselves for the worst. Sister Agnes gently removed a surprisingly clean blanket from around the baby. Lifting the infant gently out of the basket, she laid it on its back. Again, they were surprised at the cleanliness of the diaper. They were even more puzzled to discover that it was not a newborn but rather a hearty baby boy that looked to be four to six weeks old.

Sister Irene gently sponged the baby while Sister Agnes used a stethoscope to listen to its heart and lungs. The baby was in unusually good health. He was well nourished, smooth skinned, had beautiful blue eyes, and blondish colored hair. Never had they received a baby that grinned and giggled through the entire exam. Sister Agnes knew that something was just not right.

While Sister Irene diapered the baby and looked for a pair of pajamas, Sister Agnes was deeply in thought over the events of the baby's arrival. The wretched looking girl that had abandoned the infant had called it evil, "the bastard son of the Devil." She and the man in the car seemed to blame the baby for their repulsive appearance. Could they have been from one of the shantytowns? Remembering her medical studies, she reasoned that the girl could have been prostituting, contracted a disease, and then infected the man. Recalling clinical identification and photographs, she justified to herself that the only reasonable answer was that they were suffering from the advance stages of syphilis. Ignorant to their plight, they blamed the baby.

Sister Irene interrupted her thoughts,

"Sister, I will take the baby to the nursery, warm some milk and see if he will take it."

Sister Agnes nodded her head in agreement as she finished securing the infirmary. Turning off the lights, closing the door behind them, they stepped out into the main room.

Suddenly the baby started to fuss. He appeared to be pointing to the top of the stairs. Almost on the verge of throwing a tantrum, he wiggled and squirmed as though trying to get out of Sister Irene's arms. Once again Sister Agnes looked to the top of the stairs. The door was ajar!

"Sister Irene take the baby into the nursery and see if he will take some milk, I will check on Sister Sylvia." Sister Irene was quick to oblige, once away from the stairs, the infant strangely became silent.

Sister Sylvia had just turn eighty-nine years old. She had been a confined resident of the convent since the day it had opened. Sister Agnes had received detailed instructions from the Mother Superior specifically outlining the care and management of Sister Sylvia. She was to be confined to her room, allowed short walks in the convent and then only in the company of another Nun. Meals would be taken in her room and she was never to converse with any one outside the Sisterhood.

Sister Agnes rapped lightly, then opened the door and entered the room. She found Sister Sylvia partially sitting up in bed. Looking in the direction of the doorway, Sister Sylvia put a finger to her lips in a gesture of silence while motioning Sister Agnes to sit down. Moving a chair along side the aged Nun's bed, she took the elders hand and held it in her own.

Her voice subtle and restrained by age, Sister Sylvia spoke just loud enough for her listener to hear.

"Yes, you did see the door open and close. The baby has a power; I felt it the minute you brought him into the convent. It rejuvenated me to the point I could sit up and move to the door. We can communicate with each other and have been doing so since you brought him into the convent. I have little time left to warn him."

Standing, Sister Agnes stood and tried to withdraw her hand.

"Why don't you rest, I have to help Sister Irene with the baby and it's almost time to prepare your evening meal."

Not wanting her to leave she held tight to Sister Agnes hand.

"Why do you think I was held hostage in a Belgium monastery for almost my entire life? Why now am I still confined to this room? It took my whole life to convince the Vatican that I was lying and had no powers. They released me only to send me to this place where I am still confined. I could of used my powers to gain freedom, but my vows to the lord forbade me to use them as a means of vengeance."

This time Sister Agnes used her free hand to remove the Sister Sylvia's grip.

"I must leave. Sister Irene will need my help."

Sister Sylvia again nodded.

"Sister, you must see that the infant learns the teachings of Christ and learns to control his powers and never uses them for personal gain. Promise me Sister. Promise me. "

Sister Agnes took her hand and wiped the sweat from the brow of her Sister in God.

"I promise I will do as you ask. Now rest. When I return, I will bring you some hot soup and bread to go with your tea. That will give you plenty of time to tell me about the powers."

With her head resting against a pillow, Sister Sylvia closed her eyes.

"I have already warned him about the dangers of ever reveling his powers to anyone, they would seek him out and destroy him."

Weak from talking she turned her head to one side and closed her eyes. Sister Agnes stood looking as the elderly Nun fell asleep. She was very much worried about her sensibilities. She would tell Sister Irene of their conversation. In her instructions from the Mother Superior, she was informed that if Sister Sylvia ever became demented that no doctor was to be called. She was to be kept locked in her room, restraints would be used if necessary, until which time she met her demise. Sister Agnes had been given a sealed envelope, which she was forbidden to open until after Sister Sylvia's death.

Sister Irene was just removing a feeding bottle from the crib that now belonged to the new arrival. Seeing Sister Agnes enter she held the bottle up for her to see.

"He took the whole bottle with out a problem, later I will try some soft boiled carrots."

The infant was the only occupant of the nursery. A clean sterile room with three other cribs the Sisters could care for four infants, if the need should arise. Sister Agnes peered over the side rail of the crib.

"What a beautiful baby, how has he been behaving?"

With no answer forth coming she glanced to Sister Irene.

"Well?"

The Sister spoke her words carefully.

"The infant has been strangely quiet. After taking his milk he rolled onto his back and has been staring at the ceiling ever since. It's like he is listening to something."

As the two nuns stood peering into the crib Sister Agnes informed Sister Irene to the status of Sister Sylvia.

"I'm afraid that she is suffering from dementia, we will have to start locking her door, she is making very little sense and told me she is conversing with the baby."

Just as Sister Irene was to respond, the infant turned his head and looked directly at both of them. Tears were streaming from his eyes. Sister Agnes felt a sudden chilling sensation.

"Sister Irene, come with me, hurry."

Crossing the main room the two sisters made their way up the stairs and into Sister Sylvia's room. She laid on the bed face down, arms stretched outward and dressed in her white under gown. The same position when she had made her vows and dedicated her life to the service of God.

Both Nun's knew that she was dead, kneeling they recited the rosary and prayed for her soul.

Chapter 5

Sister Agnes sat alone at the kitchen table drinking a cup of hot tea. It had been three weeks since Sister Sylvia had passed away and it was a difficult memory for her to put aside.

After praying for her soul, the sister's had folded Sister Sylvia's arms over her chest, so her rosary could be placed around both hands. Wrapping her remains in a white sheet they recited one last prayer and left the room.

Descending the stairs, they crossed the visitors' room and entered the convent's main office. Sister Agnes went to her safe and retrieved the sealed envelope concerning the disposition of Sister Sylvia's remains.

Surprisingly, the letter contained a cover page, stating that she alone was to carry out the enclosed instructions Sister Irene was not to be involved or informed of the letter's contents.

"Sister Irene, I have been instructed by the Mother Superior that I alone will carry out Sister Sylvia's final arrangements. You are not to be involved"

"As you wish, Sister. I will go to the nursery and check on the baby." Nodding her approval, she smiled and waited for Sister Irene to leave the room.

The instructions were rather simple and to the point. Sister Agnes was to contact the local undertaker to handle the arrangements. There was to be no embalming. A simple wooden casket would be sufficient and a flat stone grave marker would read, "Sister S. Servant of the Lord." She was to be put to rest within 24 hours. A priest was not available; therefore no wake or church service would be held. Sister Agnes was to be the only one present at the interment and would recite the prayers of burial. The location of the gravesite would not be recorded or revealed. The letter had been signed by the Mother Superior, and oddly enough, cosigned by a Vatican Official.

The instructions were carried out as written. Sister Agnes, the local undertaker, and the gravedigger were the only three in attendance. Reading from the Book of Scriptures, Sister Agnes recited the appropriate prayers. The gravedigger and the undertaker lowered the wooden coffin into the ground.

Leaving the gravesite Sister Agnes stood waiting for the undertaker to give her a ride back to the convent. She could not help wondering what offense Sister Sylvia had committed to bring her sisterhood to such a low status. She had been banned from ever receiving the Eucharist, and not having a priest to perform the burial rites would indicate that the Vatican no longer recognized her as a Catholic Nun.

Hearing Sister Irene arriving, Sister Agnes stood and put her cup in the sink. The truth was, that she would never know the facts surrounding Sister Sylvia's circumstances. It was time to put the matter to rest and concentrate on her own service to the Lord.

Chapter 6

The word spread rapidly throughout the local area that St. Matthew's took in a baby boy that would soon be placed for adoption. Inquiries of all sorts began arriving at the convent, asking general questions on how to apply, what were the procedures, and how to obtain the necessary documents from the state. Farmers preferred older children, as they could start helping immediately with some of the lighter chores. Still, the adoption of a male infant was a very good investment for the future.

Sister Agnes, assessing the letters, was pleased that just about all of the families applying would make good adoptive parents. The child would be raised in a farm life environment, surrounded by a great deal of love, attention, and activity. It was not surprising that no one had applied in person. Most Lutheran families would prefer to handle the whole process by mail rather then have to confront the nuns personally. The sisters answered every letter faithfully, giving detailed instructions on each step of the process. Completing the personal income forms required by the state was the most complicated phase of the application process.

The Sisters invited any family having difficulty to visit the convent and they would ensure that their forms were filled out correctly. Once the application was sent to the state offices in St. Paul, it would be almost impossible to have them changed. As expected, no one took advantage of the offer.

The time frame for the adoption of an infant was quite lengthy, as the bureaucracy concerning adoption in Minnesota was very thorough. The state would take into consideration the recommendations of the sisters, but it was they who would ultimately decide to which family the baby would go.

First came a four-week search for the real parents. If that proved to be unsuccessful, the authorities would proceed to make the infant a ward of the state with the title of "Orphan Infant."

A very overworked state inspector visited Whitefield and interviewed the two sisters on how and when the infant was left at St. Matthew's. Knowing both sisters well and satisfied with their report, he cut his time short and set out for Whitefield's town office. Mainly, he questioned town authorities and a few of the local citizens as to whether they knew of any unusual events concerning childbirth. The town clerk had a report from an Army sergeant from Fort Ripley who had reported that the couple running the Trading Post at Lake Red had obtained a baby from a shantytown lady and apparently left the area. To the inspector, it made perfect sense. They had to flee before the state became aware and took the infant away from them. This was standard practice for people obtaining illegal babies. No one had any notion as to whom the parents could be who left the baby at the convent. The inspector ended his investigation and headed back to the capital.

Sister Agnes and Sister Irene were appointed the legal guardians and custody was remanded to the Catholic Church at St. Matthew's Convent. The sisters eagerly accepted the responsibilities. Their goal was to ensure that the adoptive baby would go to a home that would provide a wholesome and spiritual way of life. One of the first requirements of the church was to give the infant a Christian name. When he was adopted, the new parents could choose to change it or let the name remain.

When the baby was put to bed, the two sisters left the nursery and retired to the kitchen for their cup of evening tea. Sister Agnes placed three blank cards and a pencil in front of Sister Irene.

"Would you like the first name or the last?"

Sister Agnes sat down, placing a large white pitcher in the center of the table and then gave herself three blank cards.

"I'll take the first name." Sister Irene was pleased to have been given first choice.

"Okay, I will take the last name. You will write a different Christian name on each card and place it in the pitcher. Remember, once a card is drawn and read, you must destroy the other two cards. You cannot reveal to me who the drawn name represents. I will do the same when it's my turn. As part of our mutual agreement, we will not discuss family or origin with each other."

Sister Irene nodded her head, wrote down three names, and put them inside the pitcher. Sister Agnes reached in and withdrew one.

"The first name is Wilfred."

Sister Agnes waited until Sister Irene withdrew her other two cards and tore them up before she placed her three names in the pitcher.

Sister Irene withdrew one of the cards.

"The last name is Magnum, Wilfred Magnum."

Sister Agnes withdrew her remaining cards and tore them up.

" I like it. It has a nice sound to it." Both sisters looked at each other in awe, when suddenly a loud giggle sounded from the nursery!

Sister Irene got up from the table.

"That Wilfred picks the oddest times to express himself. I'll go to the nursery and check on him."

Sister Agnes was thinking about what Sister Sylvia had told her.

"He's special!"

Standing she put the pitcher away.

"A coincidence. That's all it is," she thought.

The following Sunday, a priest arrived from Duluth to hear the sisters' confessions and to celebrate mass in the convent's chapel. Immediately following the mass, Wilfred Magnum, screaming and crying, passed through the Sacrament of Baptism. In the eyes of the Lord and the church, Wilfred was now a Catholic.

Chapter 7

Wilfred Magnum had been at the convent for a little over three months, when Sister Agnes received notification from the Minnesota State Department of Welfare that a decision for adoption of Wilfred had been reached. It was based upon the recommendations of both Sister Agnes and Sister Irene, plus the state's thorough investigation of the family submitting the application.

Carl and Emily Sorenson, RFD2, Whitefield, Minnesota, were legally approved to adopt the male Infant, referred to as "Orphan Infant aka Wilfred Magnum" being temporary housed at the St. Matthew's Convent, Whitefield, Minnesota.

For their pre-adoptive interview, Sister Agnes was forced to meet the Sorenson family at the Whitefield town office. They had expressed to the authorities that they would not feel at ease inside a catholic convent. Sister Agnes was glad to oblige. As a family unit, the Sorenson's were ideally suited to adopt Wilfred.

Carl Sorenson, his wife Emily and two daughters, Elena who was eleven years old and Sara who was five, were the owners of a sixty-acre dairy farm located about ten miles northeast of Whitefield. September 9th, 1939 was a very exciting day for the Sorenson's. It was the day they would travel to the convent and return home with their new son and their daughter's new brother.

At the convent, it was quite another story. Sister Irene had packed Wilfred's bag with his blanket, a quilted cover that she had knitted, feeding bottles and a sizeable amount of diapers. At eleven o'clock, Sister Agnes brought Wilfred into the main visitors room where they met Sister Agnes with his fully stuffed bag.

It was the first time they had heard the baby cry in quite a while. It grew in crescendo until Wilfred was actually screaming and throwing a tantrum. Sister Agnes cradled him in her arms and spoke very softly.

"It's okay, Wilfred, you are going to a good home and a wonderful life. We will pray for your happiness and ask the lord to keep you in his care."

Wilfred stopped crying and was staring up at her when the doorbell rang, announcing the arrival of the Sorenson's. In her heart, Sister Agnes knew that she had done what was right for

Wilfred, but she dreaded the thought that he would be raised in a home that followed the teachings of the excommunicated fanatic, Martin Luther.

Holding little Wilfred close for the last time, she made the sign of the cross.

"You are and always will be a catholic. When the time comes for you to depart this world for the Kingdom of Heaven, you will see that it is a place noticeably absent of Lutherans!"

Handing the baby over to a grinning Sister Irene, she went to answer the door. The legal documents signed, the Sorenson's were given the bassinet filled with clothing articles that the two sisters had knitted and crocheted during Wilfred's stay. He was wrapped in a beautiful knitted travel blanket and placed in the arms of Emily Sorenson.

With their eyes moist, the nuns said their final goodbye and the Sorenson family left the convent with their new son. On the return trip home, Emily rode in the front seat and laid Wilfred on her lap. Elena and Sara were all smiles as they peered over the front seat to get a good look at their baby brother. Wilfred's eyes were open. Emily held him upward.

"Look at his crystal blue eyes, what a handsome baby."

Still holding the infant upward, she carefully studied the baby's features.

"Wilfred Magnum, can you believe such a name?"

Speaking to her husband, Emily turned her head so that the two girls would hear her every word.

"I already have the application to change his name. All we have to do is write his new name on the form and send it back. It's that easy."

Still examining her new son's face she was startled when his bottom lip curled upward, giving her what appeared to be a mean, cynical look. She patted his back gently, thinking that he must have a little gas on his stomach.

"Carl, why don't we name him Frank Eli Sorenson, in honor of your late grandfather?"

Taking his eyes off the road for just a second, he looked at his wife and his new son.

"That would be just fine, Emily. Thank you for remembering him."

Turning her head toward the back seat, she announced, "Okay girls, you can call your brother by his new first name, "Frankie." Your great grandfather, Frank Eli Sorenson, made it possible for your father and mother to come to America. He paid our way and arranged for us to buy our farm. This will be a wonderful way to keep his memory alive."

For a moment, all was silent in the car. Carl Sorenson had reached over and placed his hand on his wife's shoulder. Tears trickled downward from the front of his face. Both girls were surprised to see their father cry. At that precise moment, a loud sound of escaping gas emitted upward from little Frankie. It was more like a mild explosion! Sara was the first to get a whiff of the smell

"Roll down the window, Papa. It stinks in here."

Both girls started laughing hysterically. Elena rolled down her back window, giggling as she looked over the front seat.

"Did he mess his pants Momma?"

Emily Sorenson was not happy. She had a warm, mushy feeling on the top of her lap. Lifting the baby up was of no help. His traveling blanket and her dress were soaked with little Frankie's expulsions.

Carl Sorenson was laughing along with the girls.

"Lord have mercy, its worse than a pig sty on a hot day in July."

Emily was not amused. She rolled down her window so she could catch a breath of fresh air. The stench was making her sick.

Elena, holding her nose, looked over the top of her mother's seat so she could look down at the baby.

"What a mess Momma!"

Little Frankie was covered in his own waste and grinning up at her.

"Momma it's all over his pretty blanket."

Taking the clean ends of the blanket, Emily attempted to clean her hands.

"It's just as well. I had no intentions of bringing the blanket or any of the things those heretic nuns made into my house." Nudging her husband with her elbow, she went on with a few more demands. "I want everything from that convent to stay outside of the house. Before you come in from your chores, I want you to burn it all, then bury it."

"I will do as you say Emily."

Carl barely got the words out of his mouth when little Wilfred let loose with his second explosion!

Chapter 8

Carl and Emily had converted a spare room on the second floor into a nursery in preparation for the arrival of their new son. Most of the furniture had been stored in the attic after Elena and Sara had outgrown its use. The girls' crib seemed to be the only place that little "Frankie" was thoroughly content. Taken out of the crib, he would cry and fuss until somebody either rocked him or put him back in his bed.

There were two recurring routines at which Frankie was very punctual. Precisely at three thirty every morning, it was "wake up" call. Screaming in a high-pitched wail, he sent vocal vibrations rebounding throughout the entire house. At exactly four fifteen, the screaming would cease. There would be five minutes of total silence, followed by one of Frankie's massive expulsions.

Carl Sorenson had to get up each morning by five a.m., seven days a week, in order to milk and feed his cows. Running a dairy farm alone was not an easy task. The girls would do their best to help out, but lately his thoughts were about the future and when his son would join him in the fields. His only choice was to work and wait. To hire drifters was risky he had two girls to worry about. He was better off doing the work himself. If only he could get some sleep.

It wasn't long before Frankie's rituals began wearing thin on Carl's nerves. Being awakened at three in the morning and again at four fifteen badly interfered with his needed rest. No matter how hard he tried, he just could not catnap.

The strong stench of Frankie's feces would permeate into everyone's bedroom. The girls, waken first by their brother's screaming, then again by the stench, would run down the stairs and out into the early morning air just to keep from throwing up.

As the weeks passed, Emily watched her husband's usual jovial attitude change to a mood of anger and frustration. She tried to keep Frankie quiet but it was to no avail. At four fifteen each and every morning his explosion would occur. The blankets, bedding, and Frankie would be saturated in a black, stinking mess of diarrhea. Emily would have to strip the crib, wash and scrub the bedding, and give Frankie a bath. The girls would hold their noses and try to help, but most of their time was spent getting ready for school. Fatigued and overworked, Emily was unaware

44

that she was being led into the destructive grips of a deep depression.

Elena and Sara were doing poorly in school. Emily had received a note from the principle stating that both girls were falling asleep in class. He was especially concerned that their school grades were plummeting downward.

Every day after school, Sara would run from the bus stop to the rear door of the house. Climbing the stairs to her room, she would look in on Frankie taking his nap. Quietly going to his crib, she would take her finger and poke him in the rib cage, then giggle when Frankie would wake up, obviously irritated.

"That's for waking me up every morning, you brat."

Giving him a better poke, she would retreat to her room and collapse on her bed, too tired to do her chores.

At the supper table, Carl Sorenson tried to encourage his family as well as himself as to Frankie's plight.

"He's only a baby. It's tough on all of us, but we have to pitch in and help. Sara, you didn't do your chores again. Your mother had to do them for you! Elena, you and Sara have to try harder to help with your brother, plus get your chores and school work done."

Emily had brought the highchair down from the attic. Elena and Sara, using a pillow, propped Frankie up. Holding hands, the family bowed their heads, praying to the Lord to bless their food. Frankie sat in his highchair between Emily and Sara. Emily excused herself to refill a dish from the stove. Frankie turned to Sara, gave her a big grin, opened his mouth, and spewed out a stream of yellowish slime, catching her fully in the face.

Screaming, Sara ran out the door to the well, drew a bucket of water, and frantically tried to wash the mushy glob from her face. Elena followed her sister through the doorway, leaned against the side of the house, and threw up.

Emily, distracted by the girls, slipped on the grease like spatter, spilling the contents of the hot dish into her husbands lap, and onto the table. By the time the Carl and Emily had everything cleaned up, it was indeed a very exhausting night for the entire family, except for Frankie, who was squealing in delight.

Emily Sorenson was trying to calm her distraught daughter as she led Sara to her bedroom. Holding her hand, she noticed that the tip of her index finger was turning black and a small amount of pus was seeping out from under the nail. After they knelt in prayer, asking God for the patience of King Solomon in dealing with little Frankie, they were actually laughing as Sara got into bed. Emily took a moment to take another look at the finger.

"It's nothing, mama. I must have of hit it against something." Sara was not about to tell her mother it was the finger she used to poke Frankie.

"Okay, young lady, but if it gets worse, you let me know." Assuring her mother that she would, Sara too was wondering about the finger.

A few days later, Sara was sent home from school with another note from the principal. Sara's finger was almost entirely black and badly infected. The school nurse insisted that Sara see a doctor before she would be allowed back in school.

Dr. Jones, the county's only doctor, came by Whitefield twice a week. Two days passed before she was seen in the clinic. The doctor was deeply concerned after examining Sara's finger. Leaving Sara in the care of his nurse, Dr. Jones took the Sorenson's aside.

"I don't know how she got infected. I can't even guess. But Sara has gangrene."

Emily Sorenson was gripped with immediate fear.

"Please, Carl, I have to sit down."

As they sat and listened, the doctor continued. " I am positive. I saw many such cases when I served in the army. It is caused by one of the few organisms that do not require oxygen to survive. It infects as it travels within the fatty tissue beneath the skin. With the absence of air, the waste from the organism causes the tissue to rot."

Emily brought her hands upward, massaging her forehead with the tips of her fingers. She could not hold back the tears. "Excuse me for just a minute."

Going to the water fountain, she took a few gulps of cool water. Opening the door to the waiting room, she looked to see if Elena and Frankie were okay. Seeing no trouble, she returned and sat back down next to the doctor.

"Can it be treated?"

"There are sulfur drugs, but most often they are ineffective. My recommendation a few days ago would have been to remove the hand. If you look closely, you can see several minute lines streaking downward which indicates the direction the infection is spreading. It has moved from the tip of her finger, past the knuckle and toward the hand. From my experience, to be sure that the infection has not spread further the entire arm must be amputated, and soon"

Carl Sorenson was speechless and Emily began sobbing.

"Mr. and Mrs. Sorenson, you must be strong. Sara has to be told of her condition, what she's up against, and brought to the hospital in Duluth. If the marks spread to her arm, then I'm afraid nothing can be done and your daughter will die.

Dr. Jones waited for Carl and Emily to gain their composure.

"I would suggest that we bring Sara back in and let me explain to her the seriousness of her infection. It will be up to you to comfort her, prepare her for her ordeal, and get her to Duluth."

The Sorenson's, saddened and disheartened, nodded in agreement.

Chapter 9

Trying to console his daughter, Carl led her back to the car. Elena joined her sister in the back seat. Holding on to each other, they were unable to stop crying. The sound of their brother's giggling came from the front seat as he sat contented on their mother's lap. The newness of having a baby brother was beginning to wear thin. They no longer liked him quite as much.

Carl was at a lost as to what to do. The upkeep of the farm had fallen off from lack of attention. Milk production from his cows had lowered to the point where the collaborative dairy agent had informed him that unless it improved, it was not worth the expense of picking up his milk.

He has noticed that Elena had begun to stutter and had picked up the habit of sucking on her thumb.

It seemed like the only contented Sorenson was comfortably sleeping on his wife's lap.

Arriving back at the farm, Carl saw that something was wrong. The corral on the side of the barn was empty. He had penned up the cows and secured the gate latch before he left. Now they were gone! Figuring out how they got loose would have to wait; right now, he had to find them. Running to the rear of the barn, he looked out into the pasture. He could see most of the herd grazing, but moving away. It would soon be dark and if left out, they would become easy prey for the wolves.

Running back, he yelled for his daughters to stay in the car. A sharp whistle brought his two dogs on the run. Frankie woke up and let go with one of his fetid bowel movements!

Carl had one chance and that was to drive the car out into the pasture and get behind the cows. Dropping Sara, Elena, and the dogs off, they could form a line and drive the herd back toward the barn.

Emily called out to her husband.

"Go! Go, Carl! I have to wash and change us both. I just can't help you."

Carl felt pangs of guilt as he saw his poor wife and the baby, both covered in wet excrement, walking toward the house.

The girls were in the back seat and the dogs scampered to join them. Elena was sick to her stomach.

"Papa, I can't stand the smell. I'm going to throw up."

Carl Sorenson had no choice but to start the car and head for the pasture. Elena could not hold back. Holding her head down, she threw up on the back floor. Sara was trying desperately to roll down her window.

"Elena, Elena, the dogs are trying to eat it! Push them away!"

Driving with one hand, Carl slapped the seat beside him.

"Come on, Molly. Get up here."

Both dogs tried to jump into the front seat at the same time. Molly fell back just as Elena barfed for the second time. Most of the vomit landed on the dog's back. Leaping into the front seat, Molly shook the putrid substance off her back, splattering the car's interior.

As Carl wiped the puke from the side of his face, he roughly pushed the dog aside. Elena was almost at the point of hysterics.

"DDDDon't hurt him, Papa! Please ddddon't hurt him!"

Sara sobbed uncontrollably. The doctor telling her that her arm would have to be amputated and now looking at it covered with vomit was a lot for a five-year-old child to bear.

Carl Sorenson stopped; the car was behind the cows.

"Girls, you've got to hurry. We can't loose the herd. Spread out and drive them back toward the barn. It's starting to get dark. I'll drive the car down the center of the field so you will be able to see."

Turning in his seat, he could see that Sara was still crying.

"Sara, can you do this?"

Not answering, Sara left the car and ran to the edge of the pasture, turning two cows in the direction of the barn. Elena, running and sucking her thumb at the same time, took the opposite side. The dogs knew what to do and went after the cows that were trying to wander away.

Full darkness had fallen over the pasture by the time they finally got full control of the herd and started them back toward the barn. Using the car headlights, Carl led the way.

As they neared the corral, the air was suddenly full of black flies. Sara in a summer dress and Elena wearing shorts were left unprotected against the fly's vicious bite. Trying frantically to brush the blood hungry flies away, the girls opened the pen gate and herded the cows inside.

Chapter 10

Emily had brought little Frankie into the house, drew warm water, bathed him and then cleaned herself up. Putting on his diaper, she heated a bottle and laid him in his crib. No sooner had he stretched out, when the loud sound of passing gas erupted across the room. Giggling, little Frankie produced another massive bowel movement. His diaper filled quickly, the overflow of the loose excrement soaked into his crib blanket and mattress.

It was more than Emily could take. Pulling the soiled blanket away, she watched as Frankie put his hands in the waste and rubbed it on his chest. The stench made her feel weak.

"I think you do this on purpose and those crazy Nuns put you up to it."

Reaching in the crib to lift him up, she was taken aback when a sudden stream of vomit spewed from Frankie's mouth, directly on to her face.

Trying frantically to wipe the putrid mess off with her hands, Emily began to sob. Panic-stricken she ran to the door. It wouldn't open! Pulling and pushing with all her might the door wouldn't budge. It was though it was locked. The sound of the baby behind her giggling drove her near crazy. Screaming and frantic, she pounded on the door.

The wetness from her eyes, mixing with the rancid mess on her face, entered the inside corners of her mouth. The taste so vile, it caused her stomach's content to catapult out through her mouth and nose splattering against the door. Gagging, gasping for breath she slid despondently to the floor, wallowing in her own vomit. The door opened!

Dragging herself across the threshold, grabbing hold of the stair rail, she managed to get herself upright. Wobbly she made her way down the stairs and into the living room. She stood quietly looking at a painting of Martin Luther hanging over the fireplace.

"The Nun's made him do it," "The Nun's made him do it," repeating herself over and over. The evening darkness arrived, she was not aware of the change.

"The Nun's made him do it."

The girls were running behind the cows yelling and screaming trying to get them to move faster. It was useless to try and brush away the black flies; they were in a biting and feeding frenzy. With the last cow herded into the holding pen, Carl yelled to his daughters.

"Get in the barn, I'll close the gate."

With little spirit left in him he joined the girls inside. Poor little Sara's skin was covered with ugly welts from the bites of the black flies. Elena was even worse, her face and arms were puffed to twice their normal size.

Shutting the barn doors behind them, they made there way up to the house and into the kitchen. Carl couldn't ever remember being so depressed. The sight of Sara and Elena moved him close to tears.

Both girls went into the living room in search of their mother. They found her, non-respondent standing in a dark corner. Her dress covered in feces and vomit, she stood staring with glazed eyes at the painting of Martin Luther.

"The Nun's made him do it!" "The Nun's made him do it!"

Elena and Sara stood horrified. Their mother disheveled and ranting was in a state of lunacy. Carl Sorenson entered the room and stood wordless, it was too much for him to comprehend. The girls were filthy, exhausted and dejected. Elena ran into the bathroom while Sara rushed up the stairs and to her room. Carl Sorenson crossed the room and placed his arm around his wife's shoulder shaking her gently. He could hold back no longer, the tears began to run down his face.

"Emily it's Carl, are you all right?" Staring into the fireplace she continue to babble.

"The Nun's made him do it." "The Nun's made him do it."

In the bathroom Elena was able to get a good look at her face. She was panic-stricken. Sores and insect bites covered most of the exposed skin on her face. Her eyes were sunken and all of her teeth were turning black. Yellowish pus was beginning to ooze from one ear. She couldn't recognize the image of herself in the mirror. Small clumps of hair had started to fall, leaving her with grape size bald spots.

Sobbing out of control she left the bathroom and started for her room. At the bottom of the stairs she was met by the sound of Frankie's giggling. The smell was intolerable. Elena hesitated, turned and went outside.

Sara exhausted laid on the floor beside her bed. Her face, arms and legs covered with insect welts. Nauseated from the smell of the old vomit stuck to her clothes she lay whimpering uncontrollably. She cried out for her mother and father, her arm had turned black, the pain was excruciating.

Carl Sorenson knew that his wife had gone mad. He also knew that he would soon loose Sara and Elena. Without his family life would be meaningless. Kissing Emily on the cheek he left the house. There was nothing else he could do for her.

Back outside he walked toward the barn. The cow's had to be milked but he just didn't care. Opening the gate to the holding pen Carl realized how foolish he had been. They should have been on their way to the hospital in Duluth but he had put the cows before the health of his daughter's and wife. The guilt fell so heavy upon him he could feel his very soul blacken.

With the gate opened he herded the cows back out into the darkness of the night. Slapping the last one on the rump he wondered if the wolves would get it. He didn't care. His head lowered he headed back to the kitchen.

"Forgive me lord, for I am not worthy."

The farms well was seventy feet deep. It was located twenty feet from the kitchen door. As he neared, the lights from the kitchen gave him enough illumination, to see Elena perched on the wells edge. Her face was so disfigured that he couldn't even recognize that it was his daughter.

As her father approached, Elena calmly stood and waved.

"Good by Papa, I love you."

Carl Sorenson waved back nodding his head that he understood. Leaning forward Elena plunged head first, into the darkness of the well.

Passing by he managed a soft answer, "Goodbye Elena, I love you too."

Entering the house, he crossed through the living room paying little attention to Emily who was still raving on about the Nuns. Climbing the stairs he went directly into Sara's room completely ignoring his son.

Finding Sara lying on the floor he sat down beside her and took her into his arms. The Gangrene had spread from her arm and into her shoulder. Sara was dead.

Reaching in his pocket Carl removed a wooden match, scratched it on the floor and watched as it flared up. Touching the flame to the bed linen, it ignited into fire and spread quickly to the window curtains.

The last sound Carl Sorenson would ever hear would be Frankie giggling in the next room.

Chapter 11

Barn fires were not unusual in the farming community. As hard as they tried to prevent their occurrence, it was inevitable that sooner or later there would be a fire. Large piles of hay stored inside for winter-feeding would sometimes combust from a physical process in which the hay would react vigorously with oxygen to ignite a flame. The urgency in a barn fire was to rescue the animals trapped inside. Most of the farming equipment was kept some distance away from the barn. Often stored under a metal roofed shed, where it would not be placed in jeopardy by a fire.

The Johnson farm was situated uphill approximately a mile north of the Sorenson's. Fred Johnson had just finished milking his cows and was finishing his nightly chores. The night was clear and he stood in awe looking up at the large galaxy of stars that filled the entire sky above him. He amused himself for a moment by picking out several of his favorite constellations. Suddenly, he saw the glow of flames erupting from the direction of the Sorenson's farm.

Running to his truck, he stopped just long enough to tell his wife to ring the operator and tell her that there was a fire at the Sorenson's. The operator would then ring up all the farms in the surrounding area, alerting them to the fire. She would also notify the Town Constable.

Glenn Cummings was putting the finishing touches to his paper work when the call came in. Wasting no time he accelerated his new 1941 Ford cruiser toward the Sorenson's. With the red light flashing from the rooftop and the siren wailing into the night, the car sent up a cloud of dust as it sped along the gravel road. Arriving at the Sorenson's farm, he was surprised to see that the fire had destroyed the house and not the barn. As he stepped out of the car, he found Fred Johnson waiting to speak to him.

"I was the first one to get here, Glenn. The house was burning like an inferno. Some of the other folks arrived and set about forming a bucket brigade, but it didn't help much. Besides something in the well kept them from getting full pails."

Cummings interrupted him, "Did you see or find any of the Sorenson's?"

Fred Johnson pointed out into the darkness of the pasture.

"Bill Stevenson and his wife found Emily out there running around in the dark. They're still with her. It looks like she's gone crazy. They had to tie her up so she wouldn't hurt herself. Every once in a while you can hear her, she just keeps rambling on about the nuns."

"What about Carl and the two kids? Did you see any of them?"

"No, I didn't Glenn. They were probably caught inside. There's no other explanation. It will be sometime tomorrow before the ashes are cool enough for us to look for any remains. The baby is out on the front lawn."

Cummings was startled. He had forgotten the Sorenson's had just adopted a baby boy.

"Who's looking after him?"

"No one, there's not a person here who will go near that baby. Ever since they brought that infant into their home, things started going bad. We all noticed it. There's something strange about that baby."

"Why do you say that Fred? I've never heard of a case where good people refused to help an Infant."

"I'll tell you why, Glenn. The baby is out on the front lawn, not a mark on him, playing with a wooden toy that Carl carved for him. He hasn't been fed or changed but he's out there smiling and giggling."

The explanation didn't sit right with the constable.

"It's not so hard to figure, Fred. As the fire grew out of control, one of the Sorenson's brought the baby out, left it and then went back in to help the others and didn't make it back out."

Cummings was still thinking.

"It could have been Emily. After getting the baby outside, the flames were too intense for her to go back in. Frighten and scared, she ran off into the pasture. The baby sure as hell didn't walk out by himself."

Several of the neighbors had circled the two men, listening to their conversation. Joseph Finn was the first to interrupt.

"We don't want that little catholic bastard here. Take him with you and be gone!"

Constable Cummings was a fair man but not one to be told what to do.

"Mr. Finn I think it is time for you to go back to your farm."

Joe Finn knew he had gone too far. The last thing he wanted was ill feelings between him and Constable Cummings.

"Sorry Glenn, guess I'm a little tense, the baby scares me."

Several other farmers nodded their heads in agreement. Scanning the group, Cummings was even more surprised to see the women agreeing.

"If nobody is going to help with the baby, I am going to have to take him to the orphanage.

Fred Johnson interceded.

"Glenn, you take care of the baby. I'll hold the fort down here. I'll get some volunteers to help watch the property tonight. After a fire, you can be sure the looters will be lurking about. In the morning, we'll take a look for the cows."

"That will do just great, Fred, but I plan on being back tonight."

Fred took the constable by the arm.

"We had best check on the baby. I'll walk with you."

Leaving the group behind, Johnson continued.

"If it were me, Glenn, I'd would take that baby to Duluth and turn him over to authorities. The word is going to spread and I do worry for his safety."

"You got a point Fred. I'll pick up my wife and drive on over to Duluth. The baby would be better off there. I will see you late morning."

As they turned the corner of the house, they saw the baby lying in the center of the lawn, still preoccupied with his toy. Fred Johnson stopped; it was as far as he was going.

"Have a safe trip, Glenn. I'll see you in the morning."

With that said, he turned and walked back toward the waiting group. He heard the constable behind him.

"Thanks Fred, you're a good man."

Glenn Cummings approached the infant, bent down on one knee, and examined the baby. There were no burn marks, his blanket was clean, a bottle of milk lay beside him, and he appeared be quite happy. There was no doubt in the constable's mind that one of the Sorenson's brought the baby to safety just as the fire was getting started.

"Okay, little fella, you're going for a ride with me."

Wrapping him in his blanket, he lifted the baby into his arms. Taking the bottle of milk, he walked to his car. Opening the passenger door, he was glad to see that at least some of the people worried enough to make a small bed on the front seat. He could lay the baby down and not worry about him rolling onto the floor. Closing the door, he walked around to the driver's side and slid behind the steering wheel. Half the night had gone by. He would be lucky to make it back before noon.

One section of the road leading back to Whitefield consisted of a straight strip for almost a mile. It was one of the places where Glenn set up a stakeout regularly to catch the local's drag racing their cars. Slowing the cruiser down, he reached above his head and turned on the interior light so he could get a good look at the baby.

"What a cute little boy you are. With that blond hair and those blue eyes, my wife is going to adore you."

Chapter 12

Glenn Cummings grew up in St. Paul, Minnesota. He was the only child of English immigrant parents. His early life passed quickly without incident and his teen years followed suite. Attending school, he excelled in his studies, graduated with honors, and was the president of his senior class. After graduation he accepted a job at a local police precinct as an apprentice trainee. Two years later he was sworn in as a junior lieutenant in the St. Paul Police Department.

Shortly after receiving his commission his parents fell ill with a severe strain of Influenza Virus. It left them frail, weakened, and without spirit. Several months later, within a few days of each other, they both passed away. The death of both parents left Glenn, the only child, in a state of deep despair and remorse. After the mourning period ended and he attended to his parent's affairs, Glenn Cummings decided that it was time for him to move on.

A fellow officer had mentioned to him that the town of Whitefield, two hundred miles to the west, was searching for a Town Constable. Taking a few day leave he drove to Whitefield and interviewed for the Job. A few weeks later he was notified that he had been accepted and could start immediately. Resigning from his post in St. Paul he packed up his new wife, all their belongings and moved to the rural area of Whitefield, Minnesota.

By a stroke of luck, they were able to purchase a small cottage and five acres of land from a Western Union worker who was being transferred to Topeka, Kansas. Both Glenn and his wife, Joan, loved the countryside. He attended to his job as the Town Constable and Joan was hired as a teller at the local bank. They were an exceptional devoted couple that shared one major desire.

They agreed that even though the day would come when they would have their own children, that if the situation should ever arise, they would not hesitate to adopt. Joan had spent most of her life in and out of orphanages, some not so pleasant. She was fortunate enough to be adopted and raised by a family who loved and cared for her. She always knew in her heart that someday it would be her obligation to do the same.

Steering the car down the straight stretch of road, he just could not resist looking down at the infant. Glenn took his finger and rubbed it across the baby's stomach.

"Are you ticklish? My goodness you'll be walking before long."

There was no expression on the baby's face at all and absolutely no reaction from Glenn's prodding.

"What's a matter little guy? Cat gotcha tongue? Don't you worry, we are going to stop by and maybe just pick up your future mother."

It would be a long ride to Duluth and back, but if Joan reacted like he thought she would, adoption was certain. Once she saw this little guy, there would be no letting him go. As though he wanted the baby to understand he continued to talk.

"It is tragic that you lost such a loving family as the Sorenson's. We will try so hard to take their place. In the meantime you will have to stay at the orphanage in Duluth for a little while."

Deep in thought over authorities he knew that could help him out, he continued to relate his plan to the Infant.

"They will take good care of you there. I know a few people so we can get the paperwork pushed ahead. It's better than being stuck back in that convent with those crazy nuns."

So enthusiastic over the baby, Glenn had not noticed that the car had drifted to the opposite side of the road and that he had reached the end of the straightaway. Regaining his senses, he tried desperately to turn the steering wheel into the curve to keep from going off the road. Frantically, he spun the car around, to recover, but he failed. It was anybody's guess whether Glenn Cumming's ever saw the oncoming milk truck, and was simply unable to just get out of its way.

The crash was head on. The mutilated body of the constable had to be pried out of the twisted wreckage. It was miraculous, but the infant was found, without injuries, lying in a patch of grass beside the road.

He was giggling and playing with the wooden toy from the Sorenson farm.

For ten dollars, the Lutherans got the undertaker to drop the baby off on the front door step of St. Matthew's Convent.

Chapter 13

For the next few years, little Wilfred was back being a ward of St. Matthews Convent. His life was rather uneventful. He went through the crawling phase and then one day began to walk. He could talk but had to be prodded to do so. He would remain strangely silent for hours at a time. The sisters took very good care of him, but no one ever came forward to inquired about adoption. Wilfred seemed quite content with the arrangement.

The lost of the Sorenson family, combined with the tragic death of Constable Cummings, convinced the locals and anyone who would listen to them that the convent's devil baby was to blame. Wilfred became taboo well beyond the boundaries of Whitefield. The saga of the mystical baby grew to such proportions that the sisters feared that some deranged Lutheran or some

69

other malcontent might try retaliation against them and the convent...

Both sisters were careful to never allow Wilfred to be outside alone. There was a small yard for him to play but he was always kept under complete supervision.

One day shortly after his fourth birthday, Sister Agnes left the kitchen for several minutes. When she returned, the outside door was open and Wilfred was gone! Rushing through the doorway, she hurriedly searched the back yard. Breathing a sigh of relief, she found him standing by the cemetery, looking at the rows of small white crosses.

Approaching, Sister Agnes was quite displeased.

"Wilfred, what are you doing out here alone? What have we told you?"

Before she could continue her scolding, Wilfred turned and looked at her with a very strange expression on his face.

"*I hear the babies crying.*"

Abruptly taking his hand, Sister Agnes led him back toward the kitchen door. Pulling back from her, Wilfred continued to repeat himself.

"*Babies cry. Babies cry, I hear babies.*"

Opening the kitchen door she forced Wilfred inside. Crossing over the threshold, he became surprisingly quiet.

"*Sister, babies stop. I don't hear babies.*"

Visibly shaken, Sister Agnes retrieved a small wooden wagon from the kitchen pantry and placed several block toys on it. Giving Wilfred the handle, she told him to forget the babies and to go play with his wagon in the visitor's room.

Sitting down at the table Sister Agnes was apprehensive.

For the first time, she began to wonder about Wilfred's abilities. Before she could ponder his behavior much further, Sister Irene entered the kitchen.

Placing a brown mailing envelop on the table, she pushed it toward Sister Agnes.

"Wilfred is asleep on his blanket, so I let him be. This came by mail. It's addressed to you from the Mother Superior."

Sister Agnes slowly picked up the envelope and examined the exceptionally fine script writing.

"This could contain our marching orders, what's in store for Wilfred and the future of St. Matthew's Convent."

The two sisters had written a special report to the Mother Superior, outlining the problems facing St. Matthew's. The convent was operating in the red and not even close to being self-sufficient. The surrounding population had decided that the infant being kept for adoption was an instrument of the devil. There had been no inquires for his adoption. It was going on four years since the baby was left at St. Matthews's, since that time no other infant or child had been left at the convent. The local people had stopped coming for medical attention and the priest from

Duluth came every other month to say mass to an empty chapel.

The Lutherans had caused no harm to them, but if it was their intention, they had successfully shunned and isolated the convent from the local population. The future effectiveness of the convent's effectiveness was unfortunately questionable.

The Mother Superior's reply was to ask the sisters for a second report with their recommendations on how she should best proceed in order for the convent to serve as a viable asset to the church.

Two weeks later, the sisters forwarded their recommendations back to the Mother Superior. They were brief and to the point. The Mother Superior demanded that reports contain only factual information with viable recommendations. Extraneous comments were not acceptable.

The report covered three topics.

Sister Agnes and Sister Irene requested transfers to assignments where their expertise in medicine could be put to better use.

Wilfred Magnum either be placed with state authorities or sent another catholic orphanage.

They concluded that only with the assignment of two full times priest's would the church be able to gain the influence needed to advance Catholicism among the area's growing population.

Chapter 14

Studying the envelope, Sister Agnes almost wished that she did not have to open it. Sister Irene took two cups from the cupboard and put a teapot of water on the stove.

"I'll check on Wilfred, then make us each a cup of hot tea."

Nodding her head Sister Agnes was glad to have a few minutes alone. Wilfred's outbursts were still troubling her. Could Sister Sylvia have been right? Did he have some type of special power? Could such a small infant be capable of inflicting the terrible evil that he had been accused of? Placing her chin on her folded arms she prayed.

"Forgive me, Lord, for having such foolish thoughts."

Blessing herself, she stood and removed the teapot from the stove. Sister Irene joined her, placing a tea bag in each cup. Sister Agnes carefully filled each cup with hot steaming water and returned the pot to the stove. Placing the sugar bowl on the table along with two spoons Sister Irene sat down.

"Wilfred must have been really been tired. He is still sleeping. Lately, he has really been fussing at naptime. It doesn't seem possible that he will be going on five years old."

Picking up the envelope, Sister Agnes sat down, unsealed the top flap and withdrew its contents.

"I guess it's time to see what the Mother Superior has in mind for us."

Opening the letter she skipped over the letterhead formalities and went directly to the subject matter. So Sister Irene could follow along with her, she read the contents aloud.

"St. Matthews Convent will be closed and the title transferred to the Diocese of Minneapolis. It will be refurbished and serve as a retreat for Catholic priests and two assigned parish priest's who will administer to the local population and the Indian reservations. The first will arrive directly to offer you assistance.

Sister Agnes Browning will serve the will of God at St. Patrick's Shelter at Bloomington, Minnesota.

Sister Irene McDonald will serve the will of God at St. Peter's Medical Center at Duluth, Minnesota.

The orphan child, Wilfred Magnum, will be relocated to St. Philomena's Orphanage at St. Paul, Minnesota.

Specific details pertaining to inventory, building closure and transfer, will be finalized and forwarded within the next thirty days."

Folding the letter and placing it back in the envelope Sister Agnes handed it to Sister Irene as she stood up from the table.

"Etcetera! Etcetera! I suggest that we go to the Chapel for prayer and meditation before we discuss our transfers and the closing of the convent."

Agreeing, Sister Irene cleared the table, put the teacups in the sink, and followed Sister Agnes into the Chapel. Neither one heard the front door open and close!

Chapter 15

Sister Irene was surprised that it had been over an hour and they had not heard Wilfred playing in the visitor's room. He had grown to a point where he was able to wake up and amuse himself or wander into the kitchen if he was hungry. Worrying that he would sleep too long, Sister Irene went to check on him.

At her desk in the convent's office, Sister Agnes was studying the letter from the Mother Superior. The transfers did not come as a big surprise. The United States had entered into war against Germany and Japan. Factories were springing up in almost every major city manufacturing products and machinery in support of the war effort. Duluth, St. Paul, Minneapolis, and Bloomington were no exception. Those cities' populations were increasing by five hundred people per week looking for jobs. Most were poor, had no money, and were surviving off various local and national charities. It was only rational that Sister Agnes and Sister Irene's medical expertise would best be utilized in the housing projects and medical clinics surrounding the factories.

"Sister Agnes! Sister Agnes! I can't find Wilfred!"

Visibly upset, Sister Irene entered the office.

"He's gone! I can't find him anywhere."

Sister Agnes' reaction was instantaneous.

"You take the upstairs I'll search the bottom floors. If we don't find him we will meet back here."

Ten minutes later, the two sisters were back in the office. Wilfred was not to be found. Sister Irene went outside to check the grounds, while Sister Agnes searched the cellar. It was to no avail Wilfred was gone.

As she crossed the visitor's hall, Sister Irene suddenly stopped and stared at lower half of the east wall.

"Sister Agnes, look at those markings"

Moving closer, they could see that a red crayon had been used to write the letters *SS* across the entire length of the wall. It was meant to be seen.

Tracing the letters with her finger, Sister Irene had a feeling of uneasiness.

"What does it mean? Who could have done this?"

Sister Agnes stood in silence. Suddenly, the shocking meaning came to her. Wilfred was missing and the letters *SS* referred to *SISTER SYLVIA!*

Wilfred had gone to the cemetery; he wanted her to know that. Visibly shaken she asked Sister Irene to call the Constable.

"Are you all right Sister? You are very pale."

"Please make the call and be kind enough to bring me a glass of water. I need a few minutes alone."

Leaving, Sister Irene nodded that she understood. Sister Agnes selected a comfortable chair and sat down. Focusing her mind on the reality of the situation it was impossible for her to conceive the notion that a toddler could leave the convent and make his way to a cemetery over two miles away. Impossible! But she couldn't get herself to dismiss it. Wilfred was not in the convent.

Sister Irene returned with the water and watched as Sister Agnes drank.

"The Constable is on his way, he wanted to know what the problem was, I told him you would give him that information when he arrived."

"Thank you Sister, I am going to get my cloak and meet him on the sidewalk. I will explain when I get back. In the mean time I need for you to continue to search for Wilfred, he could be playing a game with us."

Chapter 16

Henry Gibson had taken the job as temporary Constable of Whitefield. Three years had passed since the death of Glenn Cummings and the Sorenson family. These tragedies were still very livid in the Lutheran community. The local populace shunned the sisters at St. Matthew's and the campaign against anyone adopting the child was still very active.

Joan Cummings had put her house up for sale and moved back to St. Paul to be near her old friends. Shortly after her departure, Henry Gibson, who had just retired from being a State Marshall, settled in Whitefield and purchased the Cummings home.

The town officials, aware of his background, approached him to consider accepting the position as Whitefield's Town Constable. Not wanting to start a second career, he agreed to take the position on a temporary basis until the town could find a full time replacement.

Thus far, it had been a relatively quiet job. The one issue that was irritating him to no end was listening to the repetitive accounts of the Sorenson fire and the exploits of the devil child. Being the Town Constable, he had to endeavor listening to the same old stories over and over.

Pulling up in front of the convent, he saw a nun standing at the roadside, apparently waiting for him. This would be his first encounter with a Catholic nun. He chuckled to himself, thinking, *"They really do look like penguins."*

Henry Gibson had no religious preferences. Since his arrival in Whitefield, several members of the Lutheran congregation had invited him to join their services. He had no quarrel with the Lutherans and found them to be a group of exceptionally devout people, but the religious bit was not for him. After declining their invitations on several occasions, they began to leave him alone. The word spread and it was soon public gossip that Constable Henry Gibson was an atheist!

Stopping at the curb, Constable Gibson stepped out of his car, came around its front end, and approached the nun.

"Good evening Sister, how can I help you?"

"If you would be so kind to let me sit in the back of your car, I would like you to take me to the cemetery on Pine Street."

Holding the back door open, Constable Gibson watched as the nun sat herself on the back seat. One of the things he did know was that nuns did not want to be touched. As he closed the door and made his way back to the driver's side, he wondered, *"Who in the hell would want to?"*

Once behind the steering wheel he turned sideways and spoke.

"Sister, can you tell me what this is about? Not many people ask me for a ride to a cemetery."

"We have a small child missing from the convent. I believe he may have made his way to the grave site of a deceased sister."

Resuming his position, he put the car in gear and slowly eased away from the curb.

"How old is this kid?"

"I don't know for sure as he was an orphan but I would say he is nearing five."

Looking in his rear view mirror, Constable Gibson slowed the car and made a second stop.

"You're telling me that a five year old kid left your convent, knew his way, and walked over a mile and a half to the cemetery?"

He kept his eyes on the nun. Her reaction was to look out the side window.

"Constable, could we please hurry? It will be getting dark soon."

Engaging the clutch, he drove toward the outskirts of town; it would take fifteen minutes at the most to get to the cemetery.

"Sister, is this the same kid that I have heard about, that he was responsible for the Sorenson's' fire and the death of the man I replaced?"

"Do you believe in such rubbish talk, Constable?"

"To tell you the truth, Sister, I don't believe in much of anything."

Turning off the road, the car passed beneath an archway and entered the Pine Street cemetery.

"Okay, Sister, where to now?"

Giving directions to the Constable, she pointed over the front seat to a nearby storage shed. "Park in front of it. I can walk from there."

Bringing the car to a stop. Henry Gibson looked at the nun in his rear view mirror.

"You got that wrong, Sister, WE can walk."

Opening the back door, he could tell that the sister was irritated by his remark. Shutting the door behind her, he stepped away from the car, making a leading gesture with his arm.

"After you Sister."

Sister Agnes was trying to get her bearings. She remembered the shed; they had passed and went straight to the back of the Cemetery. Sister Sylvia was buried almost in the woods to the side of the main part of the cemetery. She remembered the burial instructions from the Mother Superior that the gravesite remain unconsecrated and far enough away as not to upset the Lutherans.

"Have it your way Constable, follow me."

Chapter 17

The road led upward on a slight grade, and then turned sharply to the right. The day Sister Sylvia was buried, instead of following the curve, the hearse had continued forward over a grass knoll and to the very edge of the woods. Leading the way, Sister Agnes followed the same route to find the obscured gravesite. Constable Gibson, falling in behind, asked a few questions but got no reply. As they approached the edge of the woods, they came upon the grave. In the center, Wilfred sat cross-legged, swaying back and forth. He seemed to be talking to the stone marker directly in front of him.

"Wilfred what are you doing here?"

Sister Agnes was relieved to find him, but she could not keep herself from becoming very distraught. Her voice was loud and harsh.

"How did you get here? Who are you talking to?"

Wilfred did not look up. His voice was clear and pronounced.

"Sister Sylvia wanted to talk to me. She told me the way."

Stepping forward, Sister Agnes took Wilfred by the arm, pulling him upright.

"That is ridiculous. No one can talk to dead people. I have had enough of your foolishness. We are going back to the convent!"

Constable Gibson stood in awe as he watched a nun in her traditional habit; remove a five-year-old kid from the top of a grave. In his thirty-year career as a state marshal, this beat all.

"Excuse me, Sister, did he say he was talking to the corpse buried in that grave?"

"Constable, do you think a five year old can talk to the deceased, buried six feet underground?"

He had to be truthful, but could not help thinking about all the stories he had heard about the devil child.

"No I don't believe he can do that."

Tugging Wilfred by his shirt, she started back across the field.

"Then if you don't mind, would you bring us back to the convent!"

Riding back in silence the Constable knew it would be pointless to ask questions. The Nun was tight lipped and she sure as hell would not allow the boy to speak. To enter the convent uninvited would require a search warrant, which would take at least two days to get from the county seat.

Watching them both go up the walkway and into the Convent Constable Gibson sat drumming his fingers against the car's steering wheel.

"How could a kid, going on five years old, find a certain grave in a cemetery over two miles away?"

As dusk began to settle over Whitefield, Constable Gibson decided to go back to the cemetery and read the inscription on the gravestone. It might give him a clue to what in hell was going on inside the convent.

Entering the cemetery, he once again, parked along side the tool shed. Taking his flashlight, the Constable began the walk up the small road toward the grass embankment. To the right side of the road was a large lot that he had not noticed on the first trip. Giving it the once over with his flashlight he was amazed by its size. Several unique gravestones surrounded a granite base supporting a statue that was easily over ten feet high. The name "Brown" was stone carved across the front surface of the granite. Gibson was bewildered as to why someone would put money into something as worthless as a statue, especially in a cemetery.

Crossing the grassy field, Gibson walked straight toward the tree line. Although darkness had settled in, there was no problem locating the grave. Using his flashlight, he walked to the headstone, bent down, and read the inscription.

SISTER S.

SERVANT OF THE LORD

DIED 1942

Moving to the center of the grave, he removed his hat and wiped his brow, speaking his thoughts aloud.

"What in the hell is this all about?"

Looking up at the dark sky above, Constable Gibson began to analyze the overall situation. Concentrating mainly on proven facts, a concept began to take shape. When the kid had been asked who he was talking to, he had answered that he was talking to Sister Sylvia. When he picked up the nun at the convent, she had told him that the kid might have gone to the cemetery to find a sister's grave.

The one thing that might be possible is that the S on the stone stood for Sylvia, but dealing with nuns he was not about to assume anything.

If there was a Nun buried here, something was very bizarre. Henry Gibson might not be the greatest believer in the world but he knew for certain that the Catholic Church didn't bury their nuns in a pauper's grave.

Dimming the flashlight he found it easier to think. In the morning he would go to the county seat and obtain a search warrant for the convent. He would also get a court order to exhume the grave to see just who was buried below him. Once inside the convent, he could check the orphan's papers and maybe just put the stories about a devil child to rest once and for all. Clicking the flashlight back on he illuminated the gravestone.

"Well Sister S. or whatever your name is, I'll be seeing you some time this week. I hope you won't mind an examination. I'm beginning to think that the devil child might just be yours!"

The whole scenario started making sense. It would not be the first time a priest impregnated a nun. The baby could have been born in the convent with no one the wiser, just another abandoned infant found on the doorstep! With her death, the logical move would be to bury her outside the cemetery and leave the last name off the stone. A few years would go by, the grave would become obscure, and forgotten. Who would ever know?

"Well, how about that Sister S? I do believe the devil kid is nothing more than a little bastard, born to a nun whore."

Constable Gibson was extremely pleased with his conclusions. There would be no problem gaining the full support of the Lutheran community once he presented his findings that a nun possibly conceived the devil child.

After their service on Sunday, he would inform the congregation as to what he believed transpired, ensuing that there would be no delay in obtaining the search warrant and the order to exhume.

Constable Gibson thought back on the late afternoon spent with the Sister.

"That snotty ass nun's attitude will make a big change when I start tearing her convent apart."

Satisfied that he had accomplished about all that he could for the night, Constable Henry Gibson turned to start back across the field. He could not budge his feet! It was as though they were stuck in hardened cement. Searching the area around both feet with the flashlight, he could see nothing that could be holding him down. He tried using his hands to help lift up his legs, but his feet would not budge. Henry Gibson could not fathom what was happening, but his senses told him he was in some sort of unexplainable danger.

The ground below him began to tremble. Unable to move, he watched as the upper section of the grave began to give way. A sinkhole materialized at the base of his feet. Looking down into its depths he was startled by a reddish glow emitting from what must be the interior of a casket.

Frantic, he tried to look away, but the same force holding his feet now held his head in place. His arm still being free, he drew his revolver and shot repeatedly at the red glow. The bullet holes caused parts of the casket lid to splinter. Forced to look down, he found himself face to face with a grinning Sister Sylvia. Her white bib and black habit were still in tact, but her face was mostly skeletal with patches of decaying skin still adhered to her forehead and cheekbones.

Fearing for his life, Gibson began to panic.

"Let me go! Oh Lord, have mercy on me."

The rotted teeth moved, turning the facial features of the nun into a sinister smile.

"It seems your out of luck, he isn't making mercy calls tonight."

Her sinister smile became a cruel sneer.

"So you think I am a whore, do you?"

Henry Gibson was screaming for his life. Dropping his flashlight to the ground, he tried wildly to forcibly wrench his foot free and instantly felt the instant pain of a dislocation. The pain was immense as he tried to shift his weight to the good ankle.

Horrid growling sounds began to erupt from the depths of the grave. Flames shot upward into the air. The intense heat blistered the exposed skin on his hands and face. He begged to be let go.

As though his pleas were heard, the opening began to slowly close. The burning flames plummeted downward, vanishing into the grave below. In the same instant, Gibson felt his right foot and neck freed from their bond. His hands badly singed, he fumbled in the darkness to retrieve his flashlight. With his eyes nearly closed, he tried to direct the beam of light at his broken ankle. Pain permeated his entire being.

"Let me go, you old hag! Let me go!"

Tears streaming down his face, he began to scream directly at the grave.

"Whore, Whore, Whore. Whore, Whore."

The hold on his foot suddenly released. Lying down on the ground, he tried to focus his eyes on his ankle. It was impossible. He was just too scared and worn out. The beam from the flashlight lit up a small area just beyond his legs. Lying on the grave, he watched in disbelief as a section of the sod parted. A hand and arm of decomposing and rotted flesh sprung upward. The skeletal hand wrapped its fingers around his broken ankle and twisted. Screaming in sheer agony, he managed to rip it loose and heave it out into the darkness.

Struggling and unsteady, he rose to his feet. Trying to use his good foot to hop on, he lost his balance, and plummeted to the ground. Gibson's only other choice of escape was to crawl across the field on his hands and knees. Sweat poured from his face, as he heard the clicking sound of the skeletal hand closing in from behind. Again, the slimy hand grabbed at his ankle and twisted. Screaming, almost loosing consciousness, he tore at the hand, throwing it back towards the woods. The putrid slime from the hand was so wretched that he vomited on himself, as he rolled down the grassy slope and onto the road.

Once again, he heard the clicking sound of the approaching hand closing in behind him. His screams echoed off the granite gravestones as though he were trapped in a canyon.

Three days passed before a hunter, using the cemetery for a short cut, found the body of Constable Henry Gibson crushed under a fallen statue in the Browns family lot.

Chapter 18

The discovery of Constable Henry Gibson's body in the Pine Street Cemetery, crushed to death under a fallen statue of the archangel, immediately became the main subject of conversation among the good people of Whitefield. State and local officials, viewing Gibson's body before it was removed, were at a lost to account for the severe burns on the Constable's face and hands. There was no evidence of a fire anywhere in the cemetery. The top of his scalp was hairless from being badly singed. His forehead, nose, and ears, being directly exposed, were deeply blackened and charred. His clothing was badly burned in the frontal areas but undamaged in the back, indicating that the flames were not prolonged, but extremely intense and destructive. The mutilated ankle was another uncertainty. It had been literally twisted off from the lower leg bones. A few strands of stretched ligaments were all that kept it from being completely severed.

The two unrelated injuries, although very serious, were not the main cause of death. Later, it was learned from the autopsy report that the statue's weight had crushed the Constables back so quickly and with such force, it instantly drove the lungs and rib cage through the chest epidermis, smashing them simultaneously against the ground.

There had been no unusual weather patterns or earth tremors that would have caused the statue to fall. When it was erected in 1939, over ten inches of poured concrete had been used to secure the statue to its granite base. Given the circumstances, nothing less than a tornado could have caused it to topple.

The statue was raised just enough to remove Gibson's remains and put them in the care of the county coroner. Unfortunately, the last survivor of the Brown family lay at rest in one of the smaller plots. The archangel would be left where she fell and eventually destroyed by vandals and souvenir seekers.

Early the next morning, the officials emerged from the town hall to announce that a meeting would be held at noon to inform the public as to their findings in the death of Constable Henry Gibson. By eleven o'clock, so many people had gathered outside the town hall that the gathering had to be moved to the town square.

Amos Smith, the senior town official, stood on a wooden bench addressing the crowd in a loud, resonant voice. Wasting no time on formalities, he beckoned the crowd to quiet down. When they complied with his request, he spoke a brief "thank you" and began reading the report.

"*The cause of the death concerning Constable Henry Gibson is mysterious in nature. The injuries he suffered, as well as the toppling of a cemetery statue, have no rational explanations. The unexplainable events surrounding the Sorenson deaths, the death of Glen Cummings, and now the death of Constable Henry Gibson led the majority of the Counsel to one conclusion.*

The number of recent deaths was relevance to cause, reason, purpose, or logic. There was neither criminal involvement nor the involvement of insane or mad individuals.

The last time Constable Gibson was seen alive was by a witness who saw him sitting in his patrol car in front of St. Matthew's Convent.

The counsel, not in total agreement, does recognize that the deaths may be related to a power beyond our understanding.

Having finished the report, Amos Smith stepped down from the bench, hurriedly made his way through the crowd and disappeared into the town hall. Behind him, he could feel the crowd becoming restless. The majority came to one quick conclusion! Constable's Gibson's mysterious and torturous death was the work of a demon from hell.

Linking the death of Constable Gibson, Glen Cummings, and the Sorenson family to the devil child, began to escalate. The sisters at the convent had reason to start worrying about their safety. Under the cover of darkness, rocks were hurled through the convent's windows, accompanied by angry shouts of warning.

Sister Agnes insisted they spend their nights confined to the basement. The night stalkers had not yet built up enough courage or colleagues to threaten the convent during the day.

The town vendors, they depended on for food and supplies, refused to deliver. The rock throwing at night continued to accelerate shattering glass throughout the convent.

Sister Agnes knew that one of the newly appointed parish priests would be arriving sometime the next day. Anticipating his arrival, she packed what personal possessions she could fit into a suitcase and placed it by the front door. Summoning Sister Irene, she instructed her to do the same and to have Wilfred prepared to travel on a moment's notice. It was imperative that their departure be quick, and hopefully undetected, leaving the instigators little or no time to interfere.

If the priest was delayed, Sister Agnes knew that the situation would soon be unpredictable. Sister Irene continually tried to use the telephone, but the local operator would not complete the connection.

It was plain to Sister Agnes and Sister Irene that the town officials were not going to afford them any protection. Vocal obscenities and stone throwing continued to intensify. The mounting sentiments against Wilfred were completely ideological to Sister Agnes. If Wilfred possessed the so-called powers, why had he not used them to protect the convent? It only enforced her belief that the accusations against Wilfred were fabricated in an attempt to defile the Catholic Church.

It didn't take long before the "believers" invaded the town proper, spreading absurd stories about the supernatural, heretic nuns and the devil's demon child. They went all out to excite and arouse their listeners to such an extent that they would want to march on the convent and forcibly seize the child.

Once in their custody, he would be taken to the town center, tied to a wooden post, and buried beneath dried hay and cut wood. A torch would set the pile ablaze, using fire to destroy the devil's evil creation. The people of Whitefield would be freed of all evil doing, as was achieved in the burning of the witches in Salem, Massachusetts.

The belief in using fire to incinerate a child to send evil back into the depths of hell was not acceptable doctrine to the Lutheran community. They refused to be involved. The agitators turned their attention to enlisting the support of non-believers and drifters from the surrounding areas. The burning would have little to do with evil spirits, but could become the biggest event in the history of the town as well as the state of Minnesota

Chapter 19

Father O'Riley drove slowly through the town of Whitefield. According to his map, it was only a short distance to the St. Matthew's Convent. He was deeply impressed by what he saw. There was no doubt that Whitefield was going to be a wonderful area in which to establish himself as a parish priest.

Taking note of the sign reading "St. Matthew's Convent," he slowed the car, entered the driveway, and stopped at the front steps. The first thing to catch his attention was that several of the convent's front windows were broken. Stepping out of his car, he also noticed a group of people milling around on the opposite side of the road. Being perplexed to say the least, he raised his hand to knock on the front door.

It opened before he could make contact. He was greeted by a distraught nun, who nervously handed him two suitcases with instructions to put them in his car and to hurry. There was no time for an explanation. Glancing at her facial expression and detecting fear in the tone of her voice he knew she was very serious. Lifting the bags, he returned to his car, opened the trunk and placed them inside. As he closed the trunk lid, the two sisters were scrambling into the back seat with a small toddler in hand.

"Hurry Father, hurry, you must drive us away now. The child is in grave danger."

Not waiting for further explanations he accelerated the car forward. Looking into the rear view mirror, the priest was startled to see several people running behind the car, trying to catch up. Speeding away, Father O'Riley could not hold back any longer.

"What in the world is going on?"

Sister Irene was quiet and very frightened. Sister Agnes was deeply alarmed by the thought that the people were actually ready to take Wilfred by force. She looked across the seat to Wilfred. He sat grinning at her while he played with his wooden toy that Carl Sorenson had carved for him.

"Father if you don't mind, I would like to wait until we arrive at St. James to explain?"

The rest of the trip was strangely quiet. Sister Irene still frighten said very little. Sister Agnes thoughts were centered on the relationship between Wilfred and Sister Sylvia. Undisturbed

Wilfred slept. Father O'Riley decided not to push the issue until the setting was appropriate.

To pass away the time, he softly sang Irish folk songs as he drove the road back to Duluth.

It was late in the afternoon when they arrived at the Diocese of St. James parish. Although the church was located in the city proper it was surrounded by a pleasant grove of trees, flower beds and well-manicured lawns.

Father O'Riley removed the bags and carried them into the inside of the parish house. Sister Irene quietly followed behind, carrying Wilfred's belongings. Taking Sister Agnes's hand, Wilfred pointed to a park bench under one of the grove trees.

"Would you like to get some fresh air before we go in, Wilfred?"

Nodding his head, Wilfred dropped her hand and ran forward to the bench. Sitting, he waited impatiently for Sister Agnes to arrive and sit down beside him.

"Do you want to know what Sister Sylvia said to me?"

Sister Agnes was utterly shocked! Wilfred's speech was more mature and deeper than was his normal voice. Trying to hold back from fright, she quietly answered his question.

"Yes, Wilfred, I would like to know exactly what she told you."

"At the convent, it was mostly about our powers. She told me that because of her vows, she could not bring herself to use them. I, on the other hand, had no restrictions, but I should always remember that they were limited to afflictions against individuals and their surroundings. She constantly warned me about using them carelessly."

Wilfred was staring straight ahead, as though in a trance.

"I took her warnings lightly. After I had rid myself of the Sorenson's, Glen Cummings put himself in position where I had no choice, but I also brought unnecessary attention to myself which, as you know, placed me in a very dangerous position. They were ready to burn me at the stake.

Wilfred placed his fingers on the back of Sister Agnes' hand. She pulled away, they felt like frozen icicles.

"When I went to the cemetery, it was because Sister Sylvia wanted to say goodbye."

Sister Agnes clutched her rosary, visibly shaken. It took all of her courage just to speak.

"She wanted to say goodbye?"

"Well goodbye and a couple of other things."

"Such as?"

"Her powers were growing weak and soon she would be resting for eternity. She wanted to tell me for one last time, if I continued to use my power foolishly, I would soon meet with certain death."

Sister Agnes started to tremble but Wilfred took little notice.

"The night Constable Gibson brought us back to the convent, he returned to the cemetery. He came up with a theory of my being her child. Not only that, he was conceiving plans to exhume Sister Sylvia to prove it! Can you imagine the town's reaction to that?"

Sister Agnes started to realize the danger she was in.

"You might not see the humor in this, but Sister Sylvia lent me a hand in getting rid of him!"

Sister Agnes began praying aloud. There was no doubt she was in the presence of a demon.

"I don't want to alarm you, Sister, but that is not going to help you much."

Sister Agnes held the cross of her rosary, looking up into the heavens; she closed her eyes and prayed.

"Please God, rid me of this demon. Send him straight back into the fires of hell."

"That wasn't very nice, Sister, let me finish telling you what Sister Sylvia said. First, she wanted me to thank you for never letting her out of her room, so she could enjoy the feeling of the ground beneath her feet and the breeze against her skin."

"I, I was told not to let her outside."

"That's just the point she wants you to remember."

Taking his hand he placed it back on her arm.

"It does upset me, but I'm afraid I have to tell you the bad news. You are about are to suffer a massive stroke. You will be totally paralyzed and your brain will barely be functional. You will be confined to bed for the rest of your life, able only to hear, but never to respond."

Screaming in fear, Sister Agnes stood, took a few steps, and collapsed. Wilfred ran across the lawn to the parish house. Tears streaming down his face, crying uncontrollably, he pounded on the door with his fist.

"Come quick! Come quick! Sister Agnes fell on the ground."

Chapter 20

Monsignor Philip Kirkpatrick, the Archbishop of Duluth, maintained his residency at the St. James Diocese. The rumors concerning the orphan child had been brought to his attention, but he had quickly discarded them as anti-catholic prejudices.

A letter received from the Bishop of the Lutheran Congregational Church assured him that the assumptions that the orphan child was responsible for the unnatural occurrences in Whitefield were unfounded and contrary to Lutheran doctrine.

With his blond hair and pretty blue eyes, it did not take Wilfred long to capture the hearts of everybody at St. James. The decision had been made that he would stay at St. James until he adjusted psychologically from the stroke suffered by Sister Agnes and the impending separation from Sister Irene.

Tearfully, Sister Irene had tried to say her goodbyes to Wilfred, explaining that she had to take Sister Agnes's place at the St. Philomena Medical Center in St. Paul. Wilfred threw such a tantrum that he cried for two days. This led to the assumption by the nuns that the correct choice had been made. Wilfred would be watched over and taken care of by the Sisters of St. James. It would take time for him to become emotionally stable.

Each afternoon, Wilfred would climb the stairs to the third floor to visit Sister Agnes, lying lifeless in her sick bed. Wilfred would take her hand in his, then bend his head as though in prayer.

When he let the hand drop, Sister Mary, who was in charge of Sister Agnes care, would approach the bed, place her hands on his shoulders and repeat her standard response.

"I know how much Sister Agnes meant to you. She can't respond or even move or shut her eyes but I believe she can hear you."

Squeezing his arm, she would move to the door.

"I'll leave you alone for a while so you can pray in private."

The sisters had provided Wilfred with a custom made chair so that when he sat down he was eye level to the bed and could look directly at Sister Agnes.

"Well, my dear Sister, where shall we begin? I know you're still mad about the stroke thing, but you would have just talked too much"

Grinning, he took her hand again.

"Although I must thank you for not letting me get burned at the stake, I should have known better. Sister Sylvia warned me again and again, but I was careless."

Moving closer to the bed, he leaned forward and whispered into her ear.

"Did I ever tell you why I couldn't help while we were being held under siege at the convent? I didn't? Well it's because I have no power when I am under the roof of a House of God."

The cynical grin returned to his face.

"As much as I would like to ease your pain, I can't. I'm afraid it looks like you will be staying here for the next ten years or so!"

Climbing down from the chair, he stood bedside the bed just as Sister Mary returned to the room.

"I'll be back tomorrow, Sister Agnes. I love you."

As Sister Mary wiped the tears from her eyes, Wilfred passed by her and hurried down the stairs.

Wilfred loved the outdoors. He would spend much of the day running and playing among the many trees and flower gardens that surrounded St. James. It was just such a day when the Monsignor approached him.

"Wilfred, let's sit for a while. I want to talk to you."

Not wanting to do so, he never the less nodded his head in agreement and sat down beside the

Archbishop. Ironically, it was the same bench that he and Sister Agnes had shared.

"Wilfred, it's time for you to move on. You must attend classes at a state certified school and be placed in an environment that will allow the possibility of your adoption."

Putting his hand on Wilfred's knee, he tried to make the young boy understand.

"By state law, it is impossible for you to stay any longer at St. James."

Pretending to be shocked, Wilfred looked at the Archbishop with tears flowing from his eyes.

"When do I have to leave? Can I say goodbye to Sister Agnes?"

Standing upright the Archbishop looked down at the sad little boy in front of him.

"Of course you can, and by the way, you are going to a wonderful orphanage in up state New York. When we go inside, I will show you where it is on a map."

Noticing the look of disapproval spreading across Wilfred's face, he continued.

"Not many people know this, Wilfred, but you will be attending the same school that I did."

Wilfred was surprised.

"That's right, Wilfred, I too was an orphan!"

Two weeks later, surrounded by the Sisters of St. James, Wilfred climbed to the third floor for the last time. Holding Sister Agnes hand as in prayer he gave her a very flirtatious wink then said his goodbye.

"Don't be walking in your sleep, those stairs are steep!"

He was placed in the guardianship of an older man, who he was to call "Brother John." They boarded a train in Duluth and Wilfred's memories of St. Matthews were left far behind.

Archbishop Kirkpatrick watched Wilfred's departure from the out side door way of his office, choosing not to be in the group waving him off. He pondered over his decision to tell Wilfred a little white lie about him also being an orphan.

Had the Archbishop carefully inspected his office he would have discovered that someone had riffled through his personal papers. Particular the newspaper clippings from a society page announcing the   birth of Philip to Joseph and Marie Kirkpatrick of Long Island, New York.

The next morning several boil like abscesses mysteriously appeared on the side of the Monsignor's face!

Chapter 21

The train ride from Duluth to Albany, New York was long and tedious for both Wilfred and Brother John. At most of the larger cities they had to change trains, spending wasted time in station waiting rooms. The depots and trains were filled to capacity. When traveling by train, only the Archbishop and his staff went by Pullman. Wilfred and Brother John, having coach tickets, had to run, push, and shove to get seats.

World War II was nearing its end. Germany had surrendered and with the expectation that Japan would soon follow, the entire country was filled with renewed expectations and hope. Excitement, like a forged brook, ran from one end of the train to the other. On several occasions Brother John left his seat, only to return thirty or forty minutes later, after what he described as a search for medicine for his upset stomach.

Wilfred could always smell an unusual odor on his breath when he returned and took his seat. A few minutes later, Brother John would lapse into a deep sleep.

The night before the train was scheduled to arrive in Albany, Brother John left his seat again to seek out medication. When he returned, the coach was dark from the overhead lights being dimmed. Sitting down, he put his arm around Wilfred's shoulder, while at the same time using his other hand to rub Wilfred's leg. Springing from his seat, Wilfred quickly made his way down the aisle to the rear of the car. He did not know exactly why, but Brother John's actions had really scared him. Later, when he returned, Brother John's heavy breathing assured him that the Brother was in a deep sleep.

With the dawning of a new day, the train finally arrived in Albany, New York. An awaken Brother John explained to Wilfred that he would assist him to the station platform, where a representative from the orphanage would be waiting to meet them. The stop in Albany was for twenty minutes, they would have to hurry, as Brother John had to re-board. His final destination was a catholic graduate school in Wellesley, Massachusetts, near Boston.

As soon as they stepped down off the train, a young man greeted them.

"Brother John, haven't seen you in ages."

"Brother Michael, so good to see you."

Setting Wilfred's bag down, Brother John quickly embraced his old friend.

"I'll be in Boston for awhile. Let's try to make it a weekend."

The conductor interrupted any further conversation.

"Gentlemen, last call. All aboard."

Without so much as a glance at Wilfred, Brother John waved to his friend, stepped up into the train, and was gone.

Finding a seat, Brother John was still elated at seeing his friend. Things were certainly looking up. Pressing his hand against his jacket, he felt the outline of his flask, tucked neatly in his inside pocket. When the train cleared the station, he made his way down the aisle to the restroom.

Once inside, he took a long hard swallow from the flask. Feeling the urge to urinate, he unzipped his trousers and stood over the commode. A surge of sudden pain caused him to look down. An opaque pustule lesion had formed over the outlet of his urinary passage. Unable to stop the passing of his urine, the pressure caused it to force its way through the blockage. Having no control over its direction, it splattered against the front of his pants, on to his shoes, and even spotted the wall behind the commode.

Pain radiated throughout his entire body. Holding onto the sink, he bit down on his lip to keep from crying out. Weeping, he examined himself. There was no mistaking a chancre. It had to be the result of his encounter with the choir director at St. James.

"That son-of-bitch!"

Putting his flask away, he tried to dry the front of his pants. He dreaded to think about the pain that would accompany his next urination. It was a long train ride to Boston!

At the Albany train station, Brother Michael picked up Wilfred's bag and pushed him forward.

"So what in hell are you grinning about, kid?"

Chapter 22

Wilfred followed along as they passed through the train station and outside to the parking lot.

"Welcome to Albany, New York, runt! What did you say your name was?"

"It's Wilfred, Wilfred Magnum."

"Well, Wilfred Magnum let me explain to you how things work around here."

Approaching what looked like an old milk truck, his escort slid the front side door open and threw Wilfred's bag inside on the floor.

"Inside and grab a seat."

Wilfred climbed into the back of the truck. Built in wooden benches ran along each side providing enough room to hold six passengers. Wilfred took a seat and moved his bag closer to him.

There was only one seat in the front and that was for the driver.

Sliding the door shut, the Brother sat side ways in it so he could look directly at Wilfred.

"My name is Brother Michael. I am the overseer of the three barracks that make up St. Luke's Orphanage. I make it a point to meet and greet the new arrivals so that they start out on the right foot."

Reaching into his shirt pocket, Brother Michael extracted a cigarette and a book of matches. Lighting the cigarette, he inhaled deeply and blew a cloud of smoke directly in Wilfred's face.

"Well, Wilfred Magnum, what am I doing?"

"You're smoking a cigarette."

Wilfred never saw the blow coming. Violence was about the last thing he expected. The open hand of Brother Michael struck him on the right side of his forehead, knocking him to the floor.

"That's not the right answer, shit head! While you under my supervision, you see nothing and you say nothing! Can you understand that concept?"

Wilfred wanted to strike back. Instead, he nodded his head in understanding. It was the first time in his life that he had suffered the feeling of pain. Raising his head, he remembered the words of Sister Sylvia.

"Be careful, Wilfred, do not use your powers carelessly for revenge. If you do, you will be found out and destroyed."

"Okay, Punk, now that you understand the system a little better, get back on your seat.

Wilfred rose and sat down. He did not like the feeling of pain. Even worse, he did not like being dominated. It took a real effort to control his anger, but he managed to remain somewhat calm.

Starting the truck, Brother Michael drove out of the parking lot and on to the main road.

"St Luke's is located eight miles from the center of Albany."

Wilfred had to slide down the bench so that he could hear.

"The orphanage has three living barracks. You will be living in number two, commonly known as the Lourdes. Each barracks is named after a miracle. I guarantee that you will need one if you cross me. Understand?"

Wilfred leaned forward to make sure that Brother Michael heard him.

"Yes I do."

"Your barracks captain is Benny Worden, frequently referred to as Bad Benny. You don't even want to find out why."

Brother Michael looked over his shoulder at Wilfred.

"It's all up to you. I pity your ass, in more ways than one, if you become a problem. Bad Benny has two mean bastards under him and their only job is making sure everyone follows the rules."

Looking up into his rear view mirror, he looked directly at Wilfred.

"Any questions?"

Wilfred shook his head.

"No Sir."

Turing off the main highway, the truck entered a long drive and pulled up in front of a row of barracks buildings. The compound had once housed a contingent of soldiers who were assigned to protect the capital city from attack by renegade Indians from nearby Canada. Once the threat was eliminated, the soldiers were transferred and the compound given to the diocese of Albany, which converted it to an orphanage.

"Okay, Wilfred, this is your home. Take your bag, go in the front door, and get checked in.

Wilfred got out of the truck, but before he had time to enter the building, the door opened and a muscular young man stepped out. Brother Michael leaned out of his truck.

"Here's the new kid, Benny. I explained the rules to him and I think he's got the idea. I would like to stop and talk but I have to go up to the office and then I have to pick up another runt coming in from Philly."

Sliding the truck door shut, Brother Michael beeped the horn and drove away.

Benny stood checking Wilfred over.

"How old are you, kid?"

Wilfred took little time in answering.

" I'm eight years old."

Adding on a year was easy for Wilfred to do. His records had been forwarded by mail and probably had not arrived yet. Besides, who would care how old he really was?

"Everyone is at morning service or class. I'll show you your bunk and locker, and you can start getting settled in."

As Wilfred reached for his bag, Benny placed a hand on his shoulder.

"You're a good looking kid. I'm sure we will get along just fine"

Chapter 23

Brother Michael was twenty minutes early when he arrived at the railroad station for his second pick up. He was some what irked, no one for three weeks and then two in one day.

Inside the station parking lot he drove to the far upper end and parked. He was pretty much alone as most people parked closer to the depot. This way the train would pass in front of him before stopping at the station giving him plenty of time to move closer to pick up his passenger.

Lighting up a cigarette he put his feet up on the dashboard, sat back and thought about meeting Brother John in Boston. In the distance he could hear the blast of the locomotives whistle as it began announcing its pending arrival. There was need to rush, he could fantasize his weekend with Brother John a while longer, as it always took five to ten minutes for the passengers to disembark.

Taking a deep drag he blew the cigarette smoke into the air and flipped the butt out on to the ground. As he shifted his legs back onto to the floor his hands suddenly attached themselves to the steering wheel.

Surprised and confused and as hard as he tried he could not pull them loose. Watching the key turn by its self and the engine start up seemed to him, the beginning of a real bad practical joke.

"Okay, Okay who's the wise guy?"

There was no answer; instead he felt his feet move involuntarily to the gas and clutch pedals, forcing them to the floor. Sweating profusely, in sheer disbelief he caught sight of the approaching train. The engine was revved up to top speed.

Brother Michael was crying and praying.

"Please God, Please, I'll be good, I promise, I promise…"

Before he could say more, in horror he watched the shifting lever move, engaging the transmission just as his foot slid off the clutch.

The truck hurdled forward at full thrust, crossing a small embankment and a mid a shower of sparks came to rest in the middle of the tracks.

The impact between the milk truck and the locomotive was not immediate. Brother Michael could look out of his side window at the front of the train and see the engineer trying furiously to break the train. When the truck had come to rest, his feet had become loose. Standing he knew he had time to leap away, but his hands were still fixed on steering wheel. It was as though someone was deliberately torturing him.

The collision was not spectacular; the train slowed but did not derail. The milk truck because of its shabby design crumbled on impact. The slowly breaking train dragged the disintegrated wreckage under the cow sill and into its heavy iron wheels. Amid the screeching sounds of metal against metal and with a multiple array of lighted sparks the train crawled to a stop directly in front of the station.

For the passengers standing on the waiting platform the view was nothing short of spectacular. With the train grinding to a complete stop, the engineer had no choice but to release the pent up pressure in the engines boiler.

The emerging flow of steam dispersed throughout the on lookers like a heavy blanket of fog. Their vision impaired, they could not see the origin of a gummy like substance that was adhering to their outer clothes.

Splattering of Brother Michaels body parts, mixed with copious amounts of his blood and body fluids, merged with the escaping steam, to spray out over the crowd like an early morning shower.

Chapter 24

Wilfred was sitting across from Bad Benny's desk, feeling very uncomfortable. He knew that this was one person he would have to be very careful with.

"Okay, Mr. Magnum, we have a little paperwork to do, but mostly you will be checking in over the next couple of days. There's not too much to it. Nobody knows who we are anyway, and few people care.

Wilfred studied the face in front of him. Its hard feature was pitted with small scars, probably the result of gang fights or being battered.

"Everyone is either at school or working. You are expected to carry your share of the load. Six months of school then six months of galley, laundry, garden or cleaning duty. Any questions?"

Wilfred had none. They both stood up.

"Good. I'll give you some bed linen to make up your bunk along with some towels, PJ's, shower

119

shoes and a packet of toiletries. That will take care of you for tonight."

Deciding not to unpack, Wilfred put his bag inside his locker. Making up his bunk, he laid down to rest and immediately fell asleep. A couple of hours later he felt himself being shaken awake. Opening his eyes and looking up, he found that he was staring into a face he had never seen before.

"Hi. I'm Donald, I'm in the bunk next to you. If you're hungry, you'd better get up. I'll take you over to the chow hall and show you around."

Inside the dinning hall, he picked up a metal tray and followed Donald through the food line. Being hungry, he was glad to be served a generous portion of beef stew and a couple of slices of bread. Sitting down at one of the several long tables, Donald introduced him around. One of the boys passed him a cold pitcher of milk and a glass cup. As they ate, they welcomed him to the orphanage, punctuated by serious warnings about Big Red and the Enforcer.

"You break the rules and you answer to them. Sometimes they'll kick your ass just for the hell of it."

After leaving their trays at the scullery, they were on their way back to the barracks when a loud bell began to toll. Wilfred stopped to listen.

"What does that bell mean, Donald?"

"It's a general call up. We have to form up in less than ten minutes in front of the administration building for a body count. Never, ever, be late!"

Forming several rows, Wilfred estimated that there were at least a hundred boys on the field. The last group running to fall in was the kitchen detail.

Donald nudged Wilfred and nodded toward the three boys taking a head count of their barracks. It was easy to distinguish the kid called Big Red and even the dark skinned Sicilian known as the Enforcer. Making eye contact with Wilfred, the Enforcer starred at him while consulting with Bad Benny. Looking up, Benny looked in his direction and nodded his head. The Enforcer continued his count.

After all the barracks commanders had handed in their reports and everyone was accounted for, a catholic priest mounted a temporary stage and addressed the boys.

"My name is Father John Tobin. I am substituting for Father O'Brien while he is away. I'm afraid I have some very bad news. Today, Brother Michael was killed in a train accident at the Albany train station. We are greatly saddened by this sudden loss."

Wilfred could hear snickering behind him. When Bad Benny cleared his throat, the snickering stopped.

The priest was trying to continue, but seemed to be losing his concentration. He motioned to one of the staff to join him. After a few minutes the priest turned and left the stage. Going to the side door of the administrative building, he appeared to be visibly shaken. A staff member took over, announcing that a special prayer service would be held in an hour in front of the chapel. Everyone would attend and everyone was to stay out of the barracks until the service was over.

"We will pray that Brother Michael's soul has entered into heaven and the Lord has greeted him with open arms."

Again the snickering started. Donald moved closer to Wilfred.

"Watch yourself around Bad Benny and his goons. Believe me, nobody is going to miss Brother Michael."

Before he could ask why, Big Red was standing in front of them.

"Donald, quit the mouth and get over to the chapel. You, the new guy, Benny wants to see you in his office."

Wilfred caught a look of concern on Donald's face. Big Red gave Donald a shove.

"Come on, girls, let's make a move."

Wilfred walked quickly across the field and entered the barracks. Knocking on the door casing, he stepped just inside.

Bad Benny was sitting behind his desk.

"Magnum, that sure was something about Brother Michael being hit by a train. Can you believe it? That had to be some kind of freak accident. I can't wait to hear the details."

Moving back in his chair, Benny pushed himself out from the desk.

"I kept you out of tonight's service. By the time it's over, it will be close to lights out and very hectic. I know you must be pretty beat."

Wilfred nodded his head in agreement.

"Your first appointment after morning mass will be with the camp nurse. She'll give you a physical, get some urine and blood samples, and check your hair for lice. When your finished, I'll have Donald take you over to the donation center and you can pick out some more clothes. Any questions?"

This time, Wilfred answered up.

"No sir, none at all."

Just as he was about to dismiss him, Bad Benny raised a finger as if a thought had just come to him.

"Magnum, the nurse is a fussy old biddy. Make sure and take a shower and scrub the hell out of that head of hair. I don't want her on my ass, understand?"

After assuring Bad Benny that he understood, Wilfred went to his bunk and started undressing. He was really glad that he had been kept out of the service for Brother Michael. Vigils and prayer services often diminished his powers. A Mass would temporarily remove them.

As Wilfred matured, he became better equipped to evaluate the extent of his powers. He was able to impose his will against anyone that could put him at risk, as well as the circumstances, objects or environmental elements that were involved in the threat. He found that he could not use his powers indiscriminately for personal pleasure and he was helpless in a house of God. Whether the threat was real or imaginary was inconsequential; it was how Wilfred perceived it.

Wrapping his towel around his hips, he walked to the end of the barracks and entered the shower room. He welcomed the thought of a hot shower and a good night's sleep. The community shower was typical of most army barracks. The open bay was eight feet wide and twelve feet long with ten individual shower components attached along the top of the three enclosed walls.

Entering the shower, Wilfred removed his towel and hung it on a towel rack. Stepping under a showerhead, he turned on the controls and began to adjust the temperature of the water. As he stood there waiting for the water to get warm, his thoughts turned to the fact that he could not stay here permanently. He had to get away from this Jesus temple.

Deep in thought about his next move, he was surprised to hear a noise behind him. Hanging up their towels were Big Red and the Enforcer. Standing nude on both sides of him, they began to tease him about his virgin butt. Wilfred tried to step away, but Big Red pushed him back under the spray of water. The Enforcer was laughing.

"This is normally where Brother Michael would give you your indoctrination, but alas, as you know, he won't be able to make it."

Big Red turned on the showers on both sides of Wilfred.

"Need just a little bit more noise just in case you get rowdy. Everyone goes through the rite, Magnum. It's just the way it is."

Every time Wilfred tried to step away, one of them would push him back. The Enforcer was enjoying every minute of it.

"Okay, Magnum, it's time to play pick up the soap!"

Twisting around, Wilfred saw Bad Benny enter the shower. He was fully aroused. Wilfred knew what he was going to do. Big Red started to close in on him.

"I'll hold him, but I'm next."

Before they could make physical contact with Wilfred, Big Red, the Enforcer, and Bad Benny were suddenly immobilized where they stood, unable to move or speak. Their eyes followed Wilfred as he walked to the doorway, retrieved his towel and wrapped it back around his waist.

Following Wilfred's glance, they watched in awe as all the showerheads slowly turned and aimed in their direction. Water began to drip from each one. As the pressure increased so did the temperature. Clouds of steam quickly filled the room.

Wilfred stood grinning, as the showerheads opened, spraying scalding water over the three immobilized counselors. The water was so hot, that it immediately began to blister and peel off the top layers of their skin.

Suddenly their arms came free and they began to thrash them wildly. The Enforcer and Bad Benny clutched at Big Red, thinking maybe he would have the strength to free them.

For a brief moment, the showers stopped, and then restarted spurting out ice-cold water. After a few minutes, they changed back to spraying scalding water. The temperature changes against the body's nerve cells had all three jerking up and down as though they were riding pogo sticks. Wilfred was relishing their muted pain. The scalding water continued to get even hotter until it reached its boiling point. Pouring down onto the bare bodies, the fat tissue on their arms, legs and buttocks began to cook. It would be impossible to suffer any greater pain.

Slumping to the floor, feet still in place, they succumbed to a welcomed death. Chunks of steamed meat fell from their bones onto the shower floor. The fluid inside their skulls bubbled from the intense heat. The eyeballs became so badly parboiled that they either fell outward and rolled onto to the floor or fell back into the skull. Later at an autopsy, the Medical examiner would find their brains shrunk to the size of walnuts.

Chapter 25

On his arrival from Rome, Father John Tobin visited with his family for a few days, before stopping by the diocese of New York City for a short visit with Archbishop Feeney. The Monsignor and Father Tobin were long time friends. Father Tobin was looking forward to his stop, the archbishop had a huge interest in the unknown and would spend hours discussing the subject. The Monsignor found the mystery of miracles and the investigation into them absolutely fascinating, but this time Father Tobin was under strict orders not to discuss his mission with anyone.

Archbishop Feeney and most of the American Bishops knew that Father Tobin was perhaps the church's leading expert on the phenomena of miracles and the supernatural. They too were of the consensus that Father Tobin would eventfully replace the ageing Cardinal Cassinelli.

John Tobin had been born in Brooklyn, NY the son of Joseph and Margaret Tobin. First generation immigrants, who both found good jobs, were able to purchase a home, raise a son and daughter and never found a good enough reason to move elsewhere.

Strict Catholics their children were reared the same way. John, becoming an alter boy and at the age of ten, was able to recited the entire mass in Latin.

John served mass daily during the years he grew up in Brooklyn. Even with school and an after hours job, he was able to meet a heavy schedule of obligations with the church. As he neared the end of his teenage years he knew that that the church would be his vocation. His parents were not at all surprised, when after a few weeks of his high school graduation, he announced that he wanted to serve Christ and was going to enter the priesthood.

He attended the University of St. Joseph's, located twenty miles south west of New York City and graduated with a Bachelor of Arts Degree in Philosophy. It would take him another four years at the Immaculate Conception Seminary at Rye, New York, to complete the required courses in theology. He majored in the field of unexplained events, involving reported miracles and supernatural occurrences.

On April 15th, 1940 he was ordained into the priesthood. He was drafted into the Army and sent to Europe as a combat chaplain. Several months later he suffered a severe concussion and serious head wounds from an incoming artillery burst. Recovering, Father Tobin was given a medical release. Still very much limited, the war raging throughout Europe, he requested assignment to the Vatican to complete a working thesis for his doctorate. There he would have unlimited access to the vaulted records stored below St. Peters Square. These records only available to the privileged few would be invaluable in his research into the actuality of miracles and the manner of the supernatural. With the war still raging around the Vatican and Father Tobin still on the mend, the request was granted.

During his second year of study, the war over, Cardinal Cassinelli began to assign him to the actual investigation of unusual religious phenomena reported within the Catholic Church. His first assignment was a small parish located in Italian mountains near the village of Sulmona.

With most of Europe in ruins, travel was difficult. He had made it to the parish but he had walked a good part of the way. The local priest, Father Ruoti had informed the villagers that Father Tobin was from the Vatican. The turn out was befitting of the pope. Father Tobin had celebrated Mass, performed three baptisms and one wedding ceremony before the church was finely emptied.

The main reason for his trip was that the small parish church was beginning to be considered a holy shrine by hundreds of worshippers. Pilgrimages were constantly arriving in Sulmona where the town would often swell to three or four times it size.

For almost a year, at different time intervals, tiny amounts of blood had been observed seeping from the hands where Christ had been nailed to the cross. Although Father Ruoti had tried to persuade the parishioners that there must be a logical explanation, the people began believing that it was Christ showing his precious blood in shame over the atrocities of the war.

The cross was attached to the wall, six feet above the altar. Periodicity it would indeed appear that a small amount of blood would become visible on the Christ hands. Father Ruoti was not one of the believers. In the secrecy of the night he had entered the church. Climbing above the altar, he took several photographs of the crucifix. The film was passed on to his bishop, who also was concerned over the number of parishioners starting to believe in the miracle.

Cardinal Cassinelli office included a complete laboratory, workshop and several skilled craftsmen and technicians. The film was developed, enlarged and the task set upon to make an exact duplicate. It was that replica that Father Tobin carried with him on his visit to the village of Sulmona.

The two priests waited until the early hours of morning when most of the village were still asleep. Locking the doors to the church he and Father Ruoti took down the wooden cross removed the figure of Christ and replaced it with the reproduction. Father Tobin was careful to place it in a cloth bag and place it inside his satchel. A few hours later he was on his way back to Rome.

The basis of the miracle was quickly discovered. Over the years the Christ figure had become unattached from the cross. Who ever repaired it had bored small holes through the hands then attached it to the cross with small tack like nails. To cover up his work he had made a paint mixture to resemble the color of the skin. The mixture had been made from a white emulsion of tree sap that was of a rubberized base. As the seasons changed the humidity would increase then decrease causing the build up of tiny amounts of liquid around the nail heads, which in turn would rust. The small sac would fill and then secrete a few drops of rusty fluid that the parishioners believed was blood. After the switch of the Christ figure the hands never bled again. The villagers waited patiently, many still paid homage, but for the church the miracle of Sulmona was closed.

It was of the up most importance that an individual of the catholic faith maintain his belief it what he perceived he witnessed. Immediately after the Cardinal reported to the office of the Holy See, all evidence of the investigation was destroyed. The miracle would forever remain a mystery.

Father Tobin during his internship with the cardinal was never at lost for a reported miracle to investigate. One of his trips brought him to the farmlands south of Rome. A farmer had reported a tomato in his garden had the perfect likeness of the Virgin Mary. When the good father arrived a crowd of people had gathered, some praying, most making the sign of the cross. It was deathly silent as Father Tobin approached the tomato. Reaching down he picked it from its stem, turned to the crowd and took a large bite. The people stood looking in awe. In perfect Italian, the priest smiled and said. "No miracle it's just a tomato!" For a moment all was quiet, than all began to laugh and gather around the priest. The Miracle of the Lady of the Tomato was over!

Chapter 26

Father John Tobin had spent nearly three years on his thesis and was nearing its completion. He had investigated a multitude of miracles, finding logical conclusions for every one of them. In every case, he reported his findings only to Cardinal Cassinelli. What action the cardinal took, he never shared it with Father Tobin. One thing Father Tobin did know was that in all of his probes, he had never found the presence of the Holy Grace.

One evening, Cardinal Cassinelli invited him to dine at a small restaurant just outside of the Vatican. Flattered, he accepted immediately. The Cardinal was in his eighty's and as a concession to what he referred to as a little arthritis, he used a hand carved mahogany walking stick. Still with his uncertain gait, the younger clerics admired him for his keen mind and quick wit.

Declining menus they ordered pasta, bread and a bottle of red wine. When the waiter brought the wine he poured a small amount into the Cardinal's glass. Taking a small sip he nodded his approval, the waiter filled both glasses and left.

Lifting his glass the Cardinal proposed a toast.

"To my official assistant."

Father Tobin was quick to lift his glass to meet the Cardinal's. As they both drank, he noted that the word "successor" was not mentioned.

The pasta arrived and they set about enjoying their meal. The conversation changed to the state of Italy's present economy and the post war effort it would take to restore some type of normalcy.

Finishing their meal, they ordered coffee and waited patiently for the waiter to clear the table. When they were alone again, the Cardinal reached across the table and handed Father Tobin a card.

"I want you to leave the first thing in the morning for the address on the card. When you get there, go to the front door and hand the card to the sister who greets you.

The cab ride back to the Vatican was strangely quiet. Finally, the Cardinal broke the silence.

"You will soon have to finish your thesis and have it accepted by the Academy of Bishops. Thus far, your writings have been remarkably good. However, your paper is lacking a very important element, which the Bishops will be looking for. "Find it!"

Stopping in front of his residence the Cardinal stepped out of the cab. Looking through the door window, he held up his hand up to the priest.

"John, be careful."

Back in his room, Father Tobin read the card. This was going to be a long trip. His destination was a monastery tucked away in the mountains of Belgium. He packed a small suitcase with just the bare necessities, plus a small packet of priestly items. In the morning, he would catch a train to Milan, cross over into France, and then on to Paris. Once there, his final long ride would be to Brussels.

The monastery was located in the mountains east of Louvain, across the Doyle River. Father Tobin found himself hiking the last mile or so. He didn't mind the walk, the scenery was magnificent and the fresh mountain air invigorating.

As he approached the Monastery, the large wooden entrance way came into view. A very old iron doorknocker was attached to the middle of the entrance door. Lifting it, he rapped it several times and waited. The monastery was home to the Sisters of Xavier. They followed a very secluded and isolated life style, as well as taking a vow of silence.

A few minutes passed and he heard the sound of a slide bolt. A small opening in the door became visible.

"Hello, my name is Father John Tobin, I have been sent here by Cardinal Cassinelli. Here is his card."

Placing the card through the opening, the bolt slid back and the large door opened. A nun dressed in what appeared to be a modification of the traditional habit, bowed and beckoned him to follow. A veil concealed her face, there by keeping her identity private.

When Father John Tobin crossed the threshold into the monastery, he felt an inexplicable sense of fear. Following the nun through a series of hallways, he actually thought he was being watched. Finally, she stopped. Pulling a small curtain aside, she showed him a small room with a wooden bench and table. On the table was a manila envelop. Motioning him to sit down, she slid the envelope in front of him.

The only source of light came from a small window near the top of the wall. The nun, anticipating his concern placed two large candles on the table, bowed, pulled the curtain closed and left.

Pausing for a second, he could actually feel his heartbeat quicken. Picking up the envelope, he read the name printed across the top.

Sister Sylvia Deschenes, Born Paris, France-Died 1942 Whitefield, Minnesota.

Turning it over and lifting the clasp, he removed the papers from inside. For the very first time in his life, he felt the presence of evil. The room suddenly smelled of rotten flesh, causing him to gag. His head jerked upward at the sound of hysterical laughter, then silence. From all his previous findings, he knew that whatever it was, it couldn't be real. There had to be a logical explanation, probably his imagination.

The light from the window was fading so he lit both candles. His hands were sweaty and shaking as he began reading.

The first page was in outline format. It gave the date, the place and time of the interview, and the name of the Vatican representative who transcribed the priest's statement to paper. Bishop Cassinelli, who was the personal representative to the Holy See, verified the accuracy of the information, based upon the knowledge and memory of the parish priest.

The last paragraph stated the reason the name of the parish and its priest were not included. There was a fear that the public's knowledge of what occurred could cause irreversible damage to the credibility of the church and be damnatory against the priest. Yellowing over the passing of time, the first page was signed by Bishop Cassinelli. The Bishops seal was imprinted over his signature. Father Tobin put the page aside and started to read the priest's statement.

Being a parish priest for some ten years I knew the history of Silvia Deschenes quite well. Frank and Theresa Deschenes, long

time members of my parish, had confided in me that they knew she had been born to a prostitute in the slums of Paris. Left on a park bench, she had been found by local authorities and brought to the St. Rita's orphanage on the outskirts of the city. Through an official contact of the orphanage Frank and Theresa Deschenes were quickly approved for the right to adopt the baby and bring her home. They gave her the name, Sylvia Marie. The Deschenes were a very strict and dedicated catholic family. I baptized Sylvia, and helped her make her first communion. During those rites she reacted in a bizarre behavior, of which I could not understand. Some time around her ninth or tenth birthday I believe she began to find out she had special powers that only worked to do bad things. It was still a mystery to her and to my knowledge the cat incident was her first live experience.

She hated the family cat because it was always scratching her. The cat became the first real test of her powers. She inflicted the cat with a small tumor on the side of its head. Within minutes, it grew to be the size of an egg. Swelling even more, the tumor quickly became the same size as the cat's head. Then it burst, spewing out puss and part ofthe cat's brain. The family pet died an agonizingly slow death.

Because of her early age Sylvia found herself having two distinct feelings. The first one was to look at the cat dying and feel not compassion but pleasure. The second was that she did something very wrong. The second prevailed. Panicking she ran to the sanctity of the church for protection.

Merely by chance, when she came in to the church I was hearing confessions. Entering the confessional booth she blurted out to me what she had done. Although I had absolutely no reason to believe her, I knew who the little girl was and did not want to offend her or her adoptive parents. The Deschenes were more than generous in their cash gifts to the church. Stepping out of the confessional, I opened her door and asked Sylvia to follow me. As we left the church and went down onto the street, a stray dog ran by. I told her to do something bad to the dog. I wanted to prove to her that she had no special powers and that she was not responsible for the cat. She took a few steps toward the dog and it suddenly turned on her growling and showing all its teeth. The dog tried to advance but was unable to move. It was like his paws were glued to the pavement. It was trying frantically to free its self, when out of nowhere a swarm of black flies appeared. They attacked the dog unmercifully, inflicting stinging bites along its head, neck, and back. The pain from the bites put the dog in such agony that he started chewing on his own legs trying to get free. Sylvia seemed to be elated! All of a sudden the dog's four legs disappeared and its body collapsed to the ground. Yelping in pain, all it could do was to roll back and fourth while the black flies kept feasting on its bloody neck and back.

I never saw the likes of one before, but a large black bird landed on the ground in front of the dog's head. The dog tried furiously to nip at the bird, but the bird was much quicker and very hungry. Within seconds it had plucked out one of the dog's eyeballs and swallowed it. I remember glancing down at Sylvia, I was shocked to see her grinning and that she actually laughed when the dog was in the most pain. I just couldn't witness the dog's misery any longer. Taking her hand we went back inside the church.

Once back, inside the first thing she asked me if it was mean enough? I knew then that I was in the presence of something very evil. I knew that any creation of Satan or even Satan himself could not harm me as long as I was inside the church.

There was no way I could hold her in the church by force. I decided to take a chance. I told her that it had been a long time since I had enjoyed anything so much. I pleaded for her to return in the morning, and that after mass she would have to promise me that she would show me one more use of her powers. In exchange I would inform her parents that she had nothing to do with the cats death. She was very pleased with the offer and agreed to see me after morning mass.

I watched her go out through the large wooden door and skip down the steps. Once on the sidewalk, she stopped to look at the dog, it was close to death. Both eyeballs were missing and blood was bleeding from the empty sockets. It had lost control of its bowels and the black flies were busy feeding on the rest of its flesh. I stepped out of the church so she could see that I was very much interested in what she had done. She looked up at me smiling; I'll never forget what she said. The words were chilling.

"Father, doesn't he look so silly?"

Chapter 27

Waving goodbye, I stepped back inside the church door and leaned against the wall, still shaken by the most sickening sight I had ever witnessed. I knew I couldn't allow myself to get inundated. Studies at the seminary had taught me to be prepared for Satan who could appear at any time, in many different shapes, sizes and forms. At that very moment I believed that the strength of my faith was on trial. There was simply no way I could have kept her confined to the church. Praying that I had made the right decision I went to my office. It took several minutes but I finally got a call through to the office of the archbishop in Paris. Speaking to an auxiliary bishop, I related my story slowly and carefully. I was informed that the bishop was out of the country and that I should immediately call the Vatican and speak to Bishop Cassinelli. Giving me the bishops phone number, I placed the second call. It was the first time that I had ever called the Vatican. It made me extremely nervous. The Vatican operator answered and asked for my number. Giving it to her, I waited a few seconds for the phone to ring, much to my surprise Bishop Cassinelli answered. I took a deep breath and nervously related my story once again, making sure to end with the fact that I had been advised to call him directly. The bishop assured me that I had made the correct decision. Holding me on the line he gave me his most important warnings. I should never make the mistake of thinking of her as a young girl named Sylvia. That she was evil, a disciple of the devil, and a demon from hell! If I should let my guard down, she would destroy me. Once inside the church she is powerless. If she started for the outside I was to stop her anyway I could. Before he hung up he reminded me that she was using her powers to show off. Because she trusted me, her main reason for returning in the morning would be to show off again, only this time I might be included! I remember the Bishop stopped talking for a few moments as he thought out just what his plan would be. He would leave Rome without delay. Flying to Paris and be at the church around six am.

After the morning mass, I was to have her come right into the vestibule with me while I changed out of my vestments. As she watched

I would tell that a Bishop from Rome was visiting and that I told him about the funny thing she did with the dog. If she wasn't to busy, he wanted to know if she could go by the office and visit with him. He would love to meet her. With that said, Cardinal Cassinelli hung up. I felt that I had done everything I could. I looked around, spotted a pillow, and threw it to one end of the couch. I remember lying down but that was it! The next thing I knew, I was being shaken a wake. It was Bishop Cassinelli. He apologized for waking me up but he wanted his plan to go perfectly.

Chapter 28

Father Tobin heard someone approaching. Looking up, he saw a nun appear at the doorway, her face veiled. She entered the room, and set a small carafe of wine, a glass, and a basket of bread on the table. Leaving two more candles, she bowed and left. The bread and wine were most refreshing. He had not realized just how long he had been sitting there. Stretching his upper body, he returned to the papers and continued to read.

After the morning mass, the plan was put into action. The bishop had brought a well-known physician with him, who prepared a special potion that he left in my care. After the mass ended, I quickly invited Sylvia to join me in the vestibule. When we were alone, I informed her that a bishop from Rome was visiting the church and when I told him about the funny things she had done to the dog, he expressed a strong desire to meet her. Excited at the thought of meeting a bishop, she agreed and followed me to the church office. The bishop treated her like royalty. Standing, he introduced himself and asked her to please have a seat on the sofa. As planned, the bishop looked at me and asked if it were possible to get a cup of hot chocolate. I informed him that it would be no problem, and knowing that it was his favorite, I had already prepared it. Then I asked him if he would mind if I joined him. He responded that he would be most pleased, and then looking at Sylvia he asked if she would like to join us also. She accepted, and in fact asked for extra sugar, which was to my advantage, as it would help mask the taste of the sedative. Within five minutes, Sylvia had fallen into a deep sleep. The bishop had everything arranged. We placed her in an ambulance and she was given a police escort to the airport. From there, the bishop informed me that she would be going to a monastery in another country. I never saw or heard of her again. I accompanied the bishop to the Deschenes home, where he informed them that the church had proof that Sylvia's soul had been demonized at birth. She had been placed in a monastery where her salvation would be assured. She would be protected from evil and would eventually enter into the sisterhood of the Benedictine Sisters. He extended to the

Potts a personal invitation from His Holiness, the Pope, to come to the Vatican for a personal audience.

The Deschenes without reservation gave custody of Sylvia to the Roman Catholic Church.

The report was dated and signed by the parish priest. Putting the report aside Father Tobin read bits and pieces of information concerning Sylvia's life in the monastery.

Sylvia Deschenes was kept completely under sedation. She was flown to Brussels and then quickly transported to the mountainous monastery, the home of the Sisters of Xavier. She was carried to a cell like room in the lower basement. The room was furnished with a small bed, a nightstand with a water pitcher and basin and a heavy wooden desk with two chairs. There were no windows and the only means of light was by candle.

When the ten-year-old Sylvia awoke and became aware of her surroundings she was terrified. Scared and frighten she made her way to the cell like door but it was locked! Crying she begged to be let out. As her eyes adjusted to the candlelight she was startled to see a nun standing outside of her celled door watching her. Lighting a candle the nun had moved to the door and spoke.

"Sylvia, my name is Sister Mary Annette, I am a member of the Benedictine Order of Catholic Nuns. I am to be your overseer. I know that you are frightened and confused. I am going to open the door and take you to another room where you can relive yourself and wash. There will be fresh clothes for you to wear and a pair of sandals. After we will have something to eat and I will explain where you are and why."

Tears were streaming down Sylvia's face.

"Where are mama and papa?"

The sister opened the door and put her arm around the young girls shoulder.

"Believe me child, they know where you are and their prayers are with you. Come we must go."

It was eight years later when Sylvia became Sister Sylvia that her cell door stopped being locked at night.

Although she had no powers, she had never been left alone for fear that the evil being within her would try and escape. She learned to share her basement cell with the rats. Up until she had taken her final vows she would catch one each Friday, skin it alive and eat it.

Prostrating herself before the Sisters of Xavier, she made a solemn oath that she would devote her life as a servant of the Lord. The Vatican, however, took a different view. Since Sister Sylvia Deschenes had been a demon as a child, it would be less than prudent to take further chances. She would stay confined inside the monastery for over sixty years. Finally, she petitioned the Vatican on her own behalf, asking that she be allowed to leave the monastery. Being aged and a sister of the Benedictine Order, the Vatican no longer considered her to be a major threat, so she was transferred to a convent in Whitefield, Minnesota, in the United States. There, she would be confined to her room for the most part, monitored closely, and not allowed to speak to anyone outside the sisterhood.

Placing the papers back in the envelope, Father Tobin stood and stretched. A variety of thoughts raced through his mind. Why did a parish priest know more sixty years ago than he did now? He was scared and somewhat shaken by this experience. Evil, although contained, had once been present here, and he could sense it.

A Nun, entering the room, startled him. Bowing, she took the envelope, picked up one candle, and gave the second one to him. Indicating that he should follow her, she led him through several narrow passageways, descending slowly to the deepest level of the monastery. At the bottom, was a small cell like room. For sixty years, this had been Sister Sylvia's home. Father Tobin stepped back, there was so much about the existence of evil that he did not know. This was proof that it exists.

There was no reason to stay there any longer. Turning, he signaled the nun that he was ready to go. She bowed and led him through the passageways to the front door. She handed him a note, which read that he was to walk back down the pathway to the open road. There would be a car waiting for him.

Stepping out into the cool night, it took him a few minutes to adjust his vision to the darkness. He took a deep breath and started his walk down the path. Suddenly, he broke into a smile. He had found it! Now he understood what the Cardinal had been trying to tell him.

Solving reported miracles with factual evidence was his forte. He took pleasure in the fact that he was able to prove that. What Father Tobin had failed to comprehend was that Christians feared Satan and their souls being cast into the fires of hell for eternity. Each individual made a choice to accept and believe, or not to believe. By praying, using the perceived miracle as a medium, the individual expressed his or her faith. It was a means to possibly communicate directly with God, that he would hear their pleas, thus assuring their salvation. The holy grace was indeed present in the soul of every believer.

As Father Tobin approached the waiting car, he was consumed by his love of God and the revelation that he had experienced. He could not explain his strong sense of awareness when he was in the presence of evil. It was something that radiated out from his very soul, part of his very being, part of Gods will for him.

Chapter 29

Highly praised by the Vatican's Counsel of Bishops, Father Tobin's thesis earned him his Doctrine degree. He had emerged as a likely candidate for bishop and the front runner to replace Cardinal Cassinelli.

It was a remarkable accomplishment for a young American priest.

When Cardinal Cassinelli asked Father Tobin to join him again for a late dinner of bread, wine and pasta, Father Tobin knew that it was possible that the Cardinal might very well give him his endorsement. It came with the first glass of wine.

"Father Tobin, I want you to know that I have recommended to the Holy See that at the appropriate time, you should assume my duties. It won't be easy as many of the old school do not want an American having access to the Pope. Don't fret over it. In the long run, they won't be able to find anyone with better qualifications or credentials. You will be given the position, and with it will come your elevation to bishop.

It was very difficult to conceal his elation, which was quickly noted by the Cardinal.

"I know I don't have to remind you that pride is one of the seven deadly sins, but I think the Almighty will forgive a moment of well deserved self-satisfaction."

Just then the pasta arrived and Father Tobin knew that was the end of any conversation as far as the Cardinal was concerned. After the meal was finished and the last glass of wine emptied, Cardinal Cassinelli called for his car. Father Tobin was a bit surprised as they always shared a cab, but at that moment it didn't seem too important. As they pulled away from the restaurant the Cardinal leaned forward a spoke to the driver in Italian. The driver nodded his head in understanding and slid the glass partition between the front seat and the back closed.

"You are to leave for America. I have booked your passage on the *SS United States* leaving Naples in two days, bound for New York City."

Cardinal Cassinelli put his hand on Father Tobin's arm.

"Through the Mother Superior of the Benedictine Sisters, I have received word that she is convinced that Satan possesses the soul of a child, in the small town of Whitefield, Minnesota. Although still hypothetical she makes a very convincing case. It will take all the courage, strength and faith that you possess to understand the reality of the truth concerning the existence of a demon."

Father Tobin started to interrupt, "Whitefield, Minnesota!" but the Cardinal quickly cut him off.

"The demon has been described as a devil child by many of the towns population including many high ranking Lutherans. If they are correct, the demon is already responsible for seven deaths. The majority of the town's people have accused two nuns, Sister Agnes Browning and Sister Elisabeth McDonald, who ran the local convent guilty of harboring the child for up to five years, knowing all the time that he was evil. Yes Father, the same convent that housed Sister Sylvia Deschenes!"

The cardinal gave Father Tobin time to grasp what he was telling him.

"Events surrounding the death of a local constable turned the people fervently against the convent. Sister Agnes afraid for her own safety, as well as Sister Elizabeth's fled, moving the child to the St. James parish in Duluth, Minnesota. It was a good move as many of the town's people were preparing to take the child by force and actually burn him at the stake. Now it appears that action could have saved a lot of grief. After their arrival at St. James, Sister Agnes was last seen talking to the child sitting on a garden bench. No one heard his or her conversation but Sister Agnes suddenly suffered a sever paralyzing stroke. Later on the gravity of the stroke was brought into question, as she had been a model of perfect health."

Looking out the window at the lights of Rome, the Cardinal continued as though he were talking to himself.

"The rector of St. James parish, Monsignor Kilpatrick came down with a skin condition thought to be leprosy after telling the boy that he had out grown St. James and would have to leave. The infection spread over his entire body. He's been confined to an isolation unit and is near death. The infection resembled the exact distortions that others in Whitefield had suffered. A Brother who had escorted the child to Albany, New York, came down with genital warts that spread over eighty percent of his body. It has progressed to the stage where his prognosis is very poor. It is like both are kept alive just to prolong their pain and suffering. An investigation revealed that the Brother's personal preference for young boys might have resulted in his affliction, and the reason for his lingering death.

Father Tobin had been listening to every word with out interruption but he could no longer contain himself.

"My God, Is there anything else?"

"No that's about it, by the way this supposed demon's name is, Wilfred, Wilfred Magnum!"

Chapter 30

Promptly at seven o'clock the boys gathered in front of the chapel for the prayer service for Brother Michael. They watched as the priest filling in for Father O'Brien again mounted the small portable platform to address them.

Peering out over the field of boys, Father Tobin did not feel the strong sense of evil that he had earlier. Previously it had been so strong that it over powered him and for the first time in his life, he had turned and ran. He could not accept that his faith had been so weak. He prayed for the strength that he desperately needed if he was to destroy evil and preserve good.

He had spent most of the previous night talking to Bishop Feeney. Knowing that Father Tobin was traveling to the mid west the bishop asked a favor, could he spend a few days at St. Luke's Orphanage just outside of Albany? The regular priest Father O'Brien had been called a way for the death of his mother. Agreeing, he had left early the next morning, only to arrive in time for the sad news of Brother Michael's death.

Raising his arms and extending his hands outward he began the service.

"I will ask Brother Thomas a friend and coworker, to speak about Brother Michael's life, his dedication to God and what he meant to all of us."

The eulogy was short and sweet. It was a known fact that Brother Thomas did not like Brother Michael and his relationships with some of the younger boys. Brother Thomas had approached Father O'Brien about Brother Michaels conduct, but had been quickly rebuked, and dismissed. Much to Brother Thomas' dismay, Brother Michaels continued his assault on the new arrivals.

Father Tobin started to feel that Brother Michael was not a favorite with the boys. Asking that they kneel, he would pray the rosary, with the boys giving the response. With the last "Amen" Father Tobin informed the boys he was on assignment from the Vatican and would they bow their heads while he gave them a special blessing from the Pope.

Brother Thomas stepped forward as Father Tobin left the platform.

"Okay Guys, it's been a long day. Lets get back to the barracks, get cleaned up and get a good nights sleep. God bless you all."

With that blessing the boys broke ranks and were on the run. In the Lourdes barracks the boys were all pushing and shoving for position. Clothes off, towels around their waist, it was a race to the shower room. Pushing and shoving to get under a showerhead it only took a few seconds before the remains of Bad Benny, Big Red and the Enforcer were noticed.

The flesh had cooled down and lay in chunks around the mounds of skeletal bones. The eye sockets in the skulls were empty, wet hair still attached to the skulls, resembled a collection of cheap wigs. Big Red's belly had split open exposing his heart, liver and kidney's, lying on a bed of intestines, in the bottom sac of the stomach.

Panic set in. Screaming and crying the boys fought to make their way out of the shower room, through the rear door and onto the grass outside. Falling to the ground in a state of semi shock, many could not control the projectile vomiting of their supper meal. Those leaving the shower were replaced by new arrivals causing even more turmoil.

Father Tobin and Brother Tomas were standing out side the chapel when they heard the commotion coming from the barracks. Brother Thomas was quickly on the run to the barracks with Father Tobin following behind. Brother Thomas made his way through the boys, many standing like they were in a trance. A few were trying to look into the shower room. Brother Thomas pushed them aside and looked in. The sight that lay on the floor in front of him was shocking. Quickly spinning around he started shoving the boys toward the door.

"Out! Out! Out! Everybody out of the barracks! No one is to come near the shower room."

Short on breath Father Tobin arrived. Brother Thomas holding his hand over his mouth pointed inside the shower room and then hurried out the door.

Father Tobin was shaken to his very soul. Never had he witnessed such a morally repulsive sight. Not even in the throes of war had he seen such atrocities. There was no sane explanation to what happened to these boys. Their deaths had to be agonizing beyond one's conception to understand. Only a demon, a disciple of Satan, was capable of afflicting such a hideous death on a human being.

Stepping away from the shower he yelled out the door for Brother Thomas. Pale and wane he returned to the barracks.

"Go call the Sheriff, tell him we have three dead boys. Get the other Brother's to get these kids in the mess hall and away from here."

Ten minutes later Brother Thomas returned. Assisting Father Tobin, they administered the last rites to the three boys.

Sheriff Burns spotted Brother Thomas waving to him as he sped onto the compound. Coming to a stop in front of the barracks he was met by Father Tobin.

"Sheriff, my name is Father John Tobin. You best prepare yourself for what your about to see."

"Sheriff Burns, Father. Don't worry about me, there's not much I haven't seen."

Taking the sheriff inside, Father Tobin led him to the shower room. The sheriff's smugness left him as he viewed the smorgasbord of flesh and bones in front of him.

"Holy Shit! Sorry Father, who or what could have caused something like this? If I didn't know better I would have to say it was the work of the Devil"

Rushing back outside, the sheriff reached through the open window of his squad car and grabbed the radio mike off its cradle.

"This is Sheriff Burns, I'm out at the St. Lukes orphanage. I want every deputy on duty out here, like now! Deputy Jackson did you read me?"

"Loud and clear Sheriff."

"Have the dispatcher get a hold of the state police, also we are going to need the medical examiner out here. Set up a road block outside the compound then call Lou Harris and tell him I need his dogs."

"Ten four Sheriff, will do."

Going back into the building the Sheriff, Father Tobin and Brother Thomas stepped back into the shower room.

"Lord almighty they look as though the flesh was boiled right off the bones. There is just no way the shower water could get that hot."

Father Tobin spoke to Brother Thomas.

"Do you know who these boy's were?"

"Yes I do Father, the biggest one there was Red Lyrick, Benny Williams is next to him and then Joseph Picalli against the corner. They ran the barracks and worked for Brother Michaels."

Father Tobin had a hunch.

"Brother Thomas, sound the recall bell and get a count of the boys. If anyone's missing let us know as soon as you can."

The bell was sounded and the count taken twice. Brother Thomas had Brother James report to Father Tobin while he tried to calm the fears of the boys. For the time being the boys assigned to the Lourdes barracks would stay in the mess hall. If need be, they could try and rest in one of the other barracks.

"Father Tobin! Brother Thomas told me to inform you that we have one boy missing. He arrived this morning, Brother Michaels picked him up and he was assigned to this barracks."

The Sheriff's interest was peaked.

"The boy is here for one day, I have Brother Michael in bits and pieces splattered all over the station depot and now three boys who were steamed to death. Do you have a name for this kid or what ever it might be?"

"Yes I do, his name was Wilfred, Wilfred Magnum!"

Father Tobin was stunned. He now understood why the sense of evil was so strong when he first stood on the platform. The demon was actually standing in front of him.

Drawing the Sheriff aside he confided in him.

"Sheriff you must believe me. Wilfred Magnum is evil. Look at the boys. Only a disciple of Satan would carry out such a horrid act. How could Brother Michaels end up under a train? These deaths could only be attributed to a devil having no conscience, guilt, or a sense of right from wrong. I was sent here from the Vatican to hunt this demon down. I must ask you to have faith in me. I have some ability to sense the devils presence. Believe me when I tell you that he is close by."

Lowering his voice Father Tobin continued.

"Sheriff if you fine him you must destroy him. He is a demon not an innocent looking kid. Tell your men not to even think about it, shoot to kill."

Sheriff Burns looked at the priest with an odd expression on his face.

"I believe you Father, no human being could be responsible for what went on in that shower. Give you my word, we'll shoot the bastard."

Chapter 31

The surge of boiling water stopped. Wilfred watched as the dripping showerheads moved and returned to their original positions. Once his naughty indiscretions were discovered and the head count revealed him as missing, it was problematic they would blame him for the melt down in the shower. It was time for him to run, to getaway, before it was to late.

Scooping up a sizeable piece of cooked flesh, he chewed hungrily on the fatty tissue and swallowed. The extra energy would help him escape. Leaving the shower room, Wilfred hurried back to his bunk. Wiping the fleshy slime off on his towel, he let it drop to the floor. Taking only a few minutes to get dressed, his suitcase would stay behind. It would only serve to slow him down.

Approaching the front entrance of the barracks, Wilfred paused and stepped inside Bad Benny's room. Grabbing a shirt off his bed and a pair of shoes from the floor, he returned to the hallway, opened the front door, and let himself out. Walking along in front of the barracks, he waited until several of the boys returning from the muster could not help but notice him. Breaking into a full run, he passed the last barracks, turned, continued along side the building, and then sprinted into the woods.

Running straight ahead through the brush for roughly sixty feet, he stopped, turned to the right, and ran another thirty feet. Retracing his tracks, he followed the same path in reverse. Stopping in the underbrush just short of the compound, Wilfred replaced his shirt and shoes with Bad Benny's. Bundling his shoes in his shirt, he dragged them on the ground for several feet and then threw them back along the path. Going to his right, he broke out of the woods and ran onto the highway. If they used dogs to track him, they would follow the strong scent into the woods and not Bad Benny's toward the highway. Staying in the woods would have been his worse move. The dogs he could handle, but bullets? They could be fatal!

Running along side of the road, he started to distance himself from St. Luke's. Twice cars came up behind him. Waving his arms and extending his thumb he tried to hail them down, but both cars sped around him and kept going. The occupants would never know just how lucky they were. Wilfred was starting to feel uncertain. Once they knew he was on the road, it would take little time for the sheriff to catch up with him. He had no choice. He had to get off the road.

Standing in front of the barracks, Father Tobin and the Sheriff watched as a motorcade of law enforcement vehicles, lights flashing and sirens wailing, sped through the compound, slowed, and came to a stop in front of the barracks. Leaving their vehicles, they gathered around Sheriff Burns and Father Tobin for a quick briefing.

"We have three dead boys in the shower room. We have positive ID on all of them by Brother Thomas. All three were residents of St. Luke's. We have one missing boy who we believe is responsible."

The sheriff turned to the priest.

"I would like at this time to introduce you to Father Tobin who is from the Vatican, you will be very interested in what he has to say. Father Tobin."

"Good day gentlemen, I am here on special assignment from Rome to find this boy and destroy him. I can only ask that you believe me when I tell you that the boy is evil, a disciple of Satan. Some of you may not believe that there are demons that walk among us. I would ask you not to take part in the search; as if you hesitate to destroy him he will destroy you. I think once you view the remains, you will agree. The scene you are about to witness is beyond our collective imaginations."

Each official stepped into the shower room and observed the pile of flesh. Tough veteran law officers, some of them left with tears, while others had to hold a hand over their mouths to keep from vomiting.

Brother James anxiously approached Father Tobin and Sheriff Burns.

"Sheriff Burns, the boys in the last barracks said when they were coming back from muster, they saw the new kid running into the woods."

Damn glad that he had thought to call in the dogs, Sheriff Burns cupped his hands and yelled toward an old blue pick up truck.

"Lou, get them goddamn dogs ready to go. Sorry, Father."

"Sheriff, remember what I told you. Don't give him a chance. You're dealing with the unknown. Kill him on sight. Take only the men with you that won't hesitate to shoot."

Brother Thomas came out of the barracks carrying Wilfred's suitcase.

"He didn't even unpack. I guess he wasn't planning on staying long."

Opening the suitcase, Lou and the Sheriff let the dogs get a good smell of Wilfred's clothing. With their noses to the ground, the dogs started sniffing. Howling with joy, they found the scent. There was no holding them back. Running down the side of the barracks, they plunged into the brush. Yelping, they followed the trail straight into the woods. Turning right, they suddenly lost the trail. Confused, the dogs split up and searched frantically for Wilfred's scent. Getting a whiff of the scent, the dogs circled and then headed for the road.

"He tried to trick the dogs, Sheriff. He's clever. He bought himself a little time, but Old Sam is on to him. The kid's on the road."

"Okay, Lou. You stay here. Can't afford you getting hurt. I'll assign one of the men to take care of your dogs."

Hearing a train whistle to his right, Wilfred ran down the bank and into the woods. Breaking out of the underbrush, he came upon a large clearing of tall swamp grass. Pushing the grass away in front of him, his feet sinking with every step, his progress slowed, but once he got past the grass, the ground hardened again and Wilfred found himself on the bank of a narrow river. The stream ran parallel with the railroad tracks in the direction of Albany, he had to cross it to get to the tracks. For the first time, he heard the baying of the dogs coming closer to him. The Sheriff would not be far behind.

Wading into the water, he suddenly found himself up to his waist. Thinking better of it, he climbed back onto the bank and slipped out of his shirt, pants, and shoes. Wiping his clothes on the tall grass and along parts of the bank, he made his way down stream. After a short distance, he stopped, thinking he had gone far enough to throw the dogs off again. Tearing the shirt up, he threw pieces in to the water to flow downward with the current. If they got snagged as they drifted downstream, it would keep the dogs confused and going in the wrong direction. Finished, Wilfred ran along side of the stream, cut left, and leaped out into the water. The current was fairly strong and his progress slowed as he waded back up the center of the stream.

The Sheriff arrived just as the dogs were jumping in and out of the water. Crossing the stream, they picked up the scent of Wilfred's clothes and started downstream. Sheriff Burns was wise to Wilfred's techniques for trying to throw the dogs off track. Yelling to the arriving deputies, he shouted out orders.

"Sam, get back out to the road and go down to the Howard Bridge. If he's headed downstream, you could see him from there. Remember, ask no questions and shoot to kill. Tony, you and Peter take the dogs and follow the stream, just in case he doubles back. It would have been impossible for him to hop on that last train but I'm taking no chances. Paul, you go back out to the road, go to the depot and have that train searched from one end to the other. Remember, shoot on sight. I am going to walk the tracks up stream to see if he went in that direction. Paul, while you're there, have the station send a pump car out for me."

Wading through water that was above his knees, the sheriff crossed the brook, climbed the embankment, and started walking up the railroad tracks. He had gone about a half mile when he looked down from the embankment and saw Wilfred slowly making his way upstream. Sure that he had not been seen, Sheriff Burns crossed over to the right side of the tracks. Looking up from the stream, the rail bed kept his movements concealed. Running alongside the track, he got well ahead of the boy. Peering down from the rail bed, Wilfred was nowhere to be seen. Sheriff Burns quickly hopped over the tracks, slid down the embankment on his stomach, and crawled to the stream's edge on his hands and knees. Concealing himself in swamp grass, he waited.

Several minutes passed before he heard the splashing of water as Wilfred approached.

"Well Son, I guess this will end swim call for today."

His revolver drawn and aimed at Wilfred's head, the sheriff made his first mistake. He failed to follow Father Tobin's and his own instructions.

"Now, very slowly, put your hands on your head and move towards me."

Wilfred, doing exactly what he was told, edged his way slowly forward.

With his pistol still aimed at the boy's head, he motioned him even closer.

"Do you know what a dum dum is, boy? No? Well, it's where I make deep cuts into the lead on the end of my bullets, so when they hit, they make a pretty big mess. Sort of like what you left back at the shower room."

Cocking the hammer back on the pistol, the sheriff took dead aim.

"I was supposed to shoot you on sight, but if you don't mind, I wanted you close enough so I could watch your head explode."

The sheriff felt the pistol turn slowly to the right, away from Wilfred. Using the strength of both hands he could not stop it. No matter how hard he squeezed the trigger, it would not release the hammer. The pistol continued to turn as his wrist and arm bent, so the barrel came around to point at his face.

"What in hell is going on?"

The rest of the sheriff's words were jumbled as the barrel forced itself against his teeth. Wilfred lowered his hands and stepped out of the water.

"Sheriff Dumb Dumb, I want you to meet Mr. Dum Dum!"

The hammer snapped forward and the sheriff's teeth disintegrated along with the top and back of his skull.

Standing over the body, Wilfred pulled off the sheriff's boots and his pants, ignoring the blood soaked shirt. They were big but with the belt he would be able to hold up them up.

By now it was quite dark, but it had turned out to be a beautiful moonlit night. It gave Wilfred enough light to be able to see where he was going. Starting to climb up the embankment to the tracks, Wilfred quickly ducked as two men calling out the sheriff's name came by on a pump cart. They stopped almost in front of him.

"Jim, there's no sign of him. We have twenty minutes to get back before the 9:05 leaves, or else we are going to be trapped on the tracks. After the train goes out, we'll come back."

"Sounds like a good plan to me. Here, let me help you pump."

Wilfred watched as the two men pumped the handcar away. Another thirty minutes or so and he would catch the train. To where, he didn't care. He just had to get far away from St. Luke's.

Chapter 32

As the slow moving freight train approached, Wilfred got in position to jump aboard. It was a dangerous move, but he had to get out of the area, and quick. The railroad men would have been tipped off by the sheriff's deputies and be looking for him. His best chance was to stay hidden but where he could easily jump. The darkness would conceal his movements and discourage anyone from trying to follow him. He didn't have to travel a long way's, just far enough to give him a little running room.

Spotting a boxcar without a locking seal on the door handle, he ran alongside of it. Sliding the door partially open, Wilfred lifted himself up and in. Lying on his back he rested, trying to catch his breath.

"Drag in them feet boy or you'll give us away. The railroaders get us, they'll beat our ass good."

The man's voice was coming from the back corner.

Wilfred rolled inside the boxcar, with his feet in the direction of the voice.

"I covered myself up with trash and they didn't see me. If you hear them up on the roof, don't even think about it, jump! They are mean bastards."

As the voice spoke, Wilfred could tell that it was coming closer to him. As his eyes adjusted to the darkness, he could make out the figure of a man crawling toward him. He felt a hand on the heel of his boot.

"Say, boy, these feel like real nice boots. I bet you stole them?

Taking hold of both boots, the man pulled them off.

"They're way to big for you. They'll fit me just fine. What else you got, boy? Any money?"

As he started to feel his way up Wilfred's leg, the two boots began to move. Startled, the man moved back into the boxcar.

"What the hell is that? The boots are moving."

Wilfred stood and looked out the boxcar door. The train was coming to a trestle that crossed over a large river. This was his opportunity. Pulling on the door until it was almost shut, he peered back into the darkness of the car.

"One of them is a Water Moccasin and the other is a King Cobra. I hope they fit."

The man screamed in agony as the two snakes inflicted viscous bites to the side of his face. Delivered with such a force their fangs penetrated the cheeks depositing the warm venom to the inside of the mouth. The moonlight allowed enough light to see the man gasping and choking for air. Wilfred stood watching with no remorse.

"Taste like chicken, doesn't it?"

Coughing up copious amounts of blood, the man's body quivered went still, and then there was silence.

Waiting until the boxcar was just on the trestle, he slid the boxcar door wide open. Grabbing the man's hands, Wilfred dragged him to the edge of the doorway and pushed him off the train. Glaring back at the two snakes, they both hurriedly slithered into the trash and became concealed. Wilfred was pleased. They would make a nice unexpected surprise for the next visitor.

Going to the far side of the train car, Wilfred took four running steps and leaped out of the boxcar. Clearing the trestle, he plunged downward into the water below.

Father Tobin left the investigation of the boy's death up to the authorities. The medical examiner had come to remove the remains and take them to the state crime lab in Albany. Doing the best he could, he distinguished each boy by the color of his hair and his bone size. He was able to put the parts into individual body bags. The flesh, transformed into a semi-solid state, had adhered to the shower floor. With the use of a snow scoop, he was able to shovel the gelatinous remains into a large tub.

After the medical examiner left, Father Tobin, Brother Thomas, and Brother James went to the shower and scrubbed every square inch with soap and disinfectant. Using a garden hose, Brother Thomas rinsed the entire shower down until it was completely clean.

After the medial examiner left, Father Tobin called the Bishop in Albany. Briefing him to the situation, he requested the aid of an additional priest, to help in counseling, and the return of the boys to the Lourdes barracks. Many of the boys who witnessed the carnage in the shower room were sure to have severe psychological problems.

The Bishop's reply was that he would personally arrive in the early morning to help. His presence alone would ensure the boy's that the church put their safety and care foremost.

Brother James had integrated the boys from the Lourdes barracks into the other three. They wouldn't open the Lourdes barracks until the following day. It was well after midnight when Father Tobin finally got everyone settled. Informing Brother Thomas and Brother James that the next few days would be devoted to helping the boys cope, they started back to their own quarters. It had been a long day.

Before resting for the night. Father Tobin sent a cable in code to Cardinal Cassinelli in Rome. It would be early morning there. The main subject of the cable acknowledged contact with Wilfred Magnum. The local sheriff and his deputies were out tracking him down. They all knew he was evil and had instructions to kill him on sight.

All he could do now was wait for the sheriff. Kneeling, he prayed that the Lord would look over and care for the boys. Lifting himself up, he sat on the sofa. It was only a minute and the good Father was sound asleep.

The next morning at Mass, Father Tobin explained to the boys that for the time being they should put their faith and trust in the hands of God and not dwell on what occurred in the barracks. The authorities would take care of the investigation. If anyone would like to talk about his grief the Bishop was on his way to St. Luke's, and would make himself available.

Father Tobin missed the point completely. There was no grief! The boy's were street wise. They had suffered indecencies and abuse under the so call tutelage of Brother Michael and his henchmen. Good riddance! Nobody, but nobody, was going to miss those creeps.

Shortly after the mass ended, he was informed that the body of Sheriff Burns had been found. It was evident that he had not followed Father Tobin's instructions nor his own and that Wilfred had escaped. The area along the railroad tracks, as well as all train cars, had been searched without finding a trace. Two railroad workers had died from snakebites while searching one of the boxcars.

Father Tobin knew immediately that Wilfred had been in that boxcar and somehow had eluded the search for him.

An early morning call had verified that the Bishop would be arriving around eleven that morning. Father Tobin met with the Brothers. The recall bell would be sounded at ten thirty so that the boys could be assembled to properly welcome him. He also instructed Brother James to set up the portable speaker platform in the event the monsignor wanted to address the boys.

Chapter 33

The river came up fast. Wilfred felt the coldness on his body as he plunged deep into the water. Surfacing, he let the flow of the river carry him down stream, while slowly kicking his way towards the riverbank. Slipping out of the sheriff's trousers, he tied the end of each pant leg into a knot. Scooping the pants out of the water, above his head, then downward, he filled the pants with air making a very usable float.

When he had distanced himself well away from the railroad trestle he let the current push him into the shore. Wading out of the water, he was faced with a twenty-foot embankment to climb. It was steep and in the moonlight appeared to have a cover of river grass and weeds. There was little to grab on to pull himself up. Crawling, he had to dig into the muck with his hands and feet to slowly edge his way upwards. With his chest and legs badly bruised he finally swung himself over the top. Exhausted and wet, he crawled under a thicket of bushes. His body well concealed, he quickly fell asleep.

Wilfred awoke to a shinning sun. Removing himself from his nesting place he carefully took a good look about. It appeared that he was in a well-populated area; he would have to be extremely careful. Wiping the early morning dew from the grass he washed his hands and then his face. The coolness of the water brought back his full awareness.

Although they were too big and soaking wet he slipped the sheriff's trousers back on and tighten up the belt. Sneaking his way a long several hedgerows he came to a back yard with a full line of clothes drying in the early morning sun. Unnoticed he stole a shirt and a pair of pants, they wouldn't be missed until well in to the day. He had no shoes, but for a youngster his age it was common and would not be suspicious. Once he found somebody with his shoe size he would rectify that problem.

Trying to find a main road he followed a path away from the river and past more houses. Behind one, he found a flourishing vegetable garden. Helping himself to the peas, carrots and red tomatoes he was suddenly startled by a women's shout.

"Get out of my garden you little tramp."

At the same time she stepped out into her yard with a broom in hand and accompanied by a very large dog.

'Sic Um Boy, Sic Um"

The dog snarling started to heed the command of its master, then stopped. Whining he tried to turn and run, the women hit him with her broom.

"Damn you I told you to get him!"

Before the dog could react, the ground opened beneath them and they dropped out of sight. As fast as the earth opened it closed! The disappearance of Mrs. Perkins and her dog Daisy would become almost legendary.

Wilfred found himself with no place to really go, having no plan he made a decision to return to Whitefield. No one would recognize him, he owed a few Lutherans a debt and that alone should make for a fun homecoming. Hitching rides on trucks and jumping on train cars he made good time and within a few days was well into Indiana. By the time Wilfred made it to Duluth, Father Tobin was just leaving Albany by train. Wilfred had a new pair of shoes!

Having plenty of patience, Wilfred concealed his presence by staying behind the large shrubs that surrounded the St. James parish house. Positioned where he could see through the windows, he was able to tell when a nun came down the stairs from Sister Agnes's room and how long it was before she or another went back. He estimated that it gave him plenty of time for what he wanted to do.

Moving closer, this time when the nun passed the window, Wilfred gently opened the front door and made his way up the stairs.

"Hello, my dear Sister Agnes, its me, Wilfred! Guess why I came all the way back here? Your going on a trip!"

Paralyzed and only having the sense of hearing Sister Agnes was unable to show any expression or reaction.

"Haven't I grown? You're not much for conversation today are you?"

Taking the bed sheet under her body he pulled it to the edge of the bed.

"Your so skinny Sister, haven't you been eating your vegetables?"

Holding the sheet and placing his arm under her back, he was able to very quietly lower the nun to the floor. Pulling on the sheet he dragged her across the room and to the top of the stairway.

"You just can't lay in bed all day, you should try and walk down the stairs."

Sitting her in an up position, he held her while he got behind her.

"I know you haven't been down stairs in a very long time. This might hurt a little bit, but you'll live. I know you have been lying in bed, day after day the same old routine. I tried to think what could I do? Then it came to me; PAIN! It will give you something to keep your mind focused."

Placing his foot against her back, he gave her a fast push forward. Sister Agnes tumbled the length of the stairs landing at the bottom on her back. Hearing the noise one of the Sisters came to investigate, gasping she turned and ran for help.

Wilfred took the opportunity to throw the sheet back on the bed, hurry down the stairs, step on Sister Agnes' chest and quietly exit out the door.

Father Tobin arrived at St. James just as the doctor was leaving.

"Excuse me, are you Father Tobin?"

"Yes I am why do you ask?"

I am Doctor Sullivan. The Sisters informed me you were on your way. I have been taking care of Sister Agnes since she had her accident. Being paralyzed there is no way she could have got out of her bed alone. If things weren't bad enough, she now has six broken bones and at her age the healing process will be slow. The Sisters here at St. James are frightened, as the incident was very suspicious. By law, I had to report it to the authorities. I hope you can help."

Huddled in the fetal position, Emily Sorenson laid in the corner of her cell. Covered in her own filth and clearly mad, she sucked on her thumb, mumbling aloud.

"The nun's made him do it."

"Mommy, Mommy, it's me, Frankie. Don't you remember me, I'm your son all most grown."

Emily's head impulsively looked upwards, she strained to look through the bars.

"Mommy you left me up stairs in the crib all alone, I didn't know what to do."

Using her legs, Emily tried to stand by pushing her back upwards against the wall.

"Did you know that poor Elena did a head dive into the well? I mean that well is over forty feet deep, she's still down there. Then there was Sara that nasty gangrene just ate her up! Then dumb Carl, my so-called father, sets the house on fire. I was lucky to get out of there. You weren't much help, out in the pasture running around like a lunatic."

Emily slowly eased her way along the cell wall as she listen to the young boy.

I mean what else could I do, you were going to make me in to a Lutheran! Frankie, what a sick name that was. All I could see coming my way in the future was cow flops and stink. "

Emily was at the cell door staring, trying to make her mouth move.

"I wish I could stay longer mommy, but I'm going out to the old homestead and get Elena out of the well. I want to prop up what's left of her so she's sitting on the edge. That way anybody that's been drinking the water will know that they are carrying a little bit of Elena inside of them. What a nice way of remembering the poor girl."

Moving a little closer to the bars he looked directly into Emily's sunken eyes.

"Well I'm out of here, but I wanted to give you something to remember the good old days."

His mouth open, a mass of putrid stomach bile spurted between the bars and directly onto Emily's face.

Turning, Wilfred walked down the hallway to the main door. A staff member let him out.

Emily Sorenson's screams could be heard throughout the institution. When the attendant arrived at her cell he found Emily on the floor. So violently had she smash her forehead against the steel bars, that her skull had cracked wide open. The brain was exposed and mixing with the strewed vomit. Already, the attendant had to shoo a way a hungry rat. Looking at the mess he would have to clean up, he decided to let the rats do it for him. He would come back in the morning. In fact it was going to be a treat not to have to listen to that, the nun's made him do it, shit anymore.

Chapter 34

Father Tobin wondered what he had walked into. Entering the Parish House living room, he found several nuns waiting to see him. With coffee cup in hand and a few brownies under his belt, he sat down and listened to the woeful story of Sister Agnes.

Introduced to Sister Irene, she did her best to describe the events concerning the convent and the mission of the two sisters.

"Wilfred's arrival was out of the ordinary as he was in near perfect health. The Sorenson family, whose home burned in a tragic fire, adopted him. Three members of the family perished. The lone survivor, Mrs. Sorenson, I am sorry to say, has been institutionalized since the fire. The baby somehow survived and was found on the front lawn. No one would go near him. The constable, who was bringing him to the state orphanage in Duluth, was killed shortly after leaving the

Sorenson's farm in a bizarre car accident. The baby again survived without a scratch. The people paid   the local undertaker to bring him to the convent. They wouldn't go near him. There was a growing belief that the baby was evil and that he was responsible for the loss of life. At first, they shunned the convent and tried to starve us out. They got braver and began stoning the building at night. They demanded that we hand over the baby so they could take him to the town square and burn him at the stake."

Sipping a glass of ice water, she cleared her throat and continued.

"Sister Agnes kept a lot of information to herself. She did not want to burden me with that for which she alone was responsible. Over a period of time, I began to feel that she was worried about some of Wilfred's behavior traits. When we arrived at St James, she took him for a short walk. When I looked out the window, they were sitting on a bench chatting. The next thing we knew was that Sister Agnes had suffered a severe stroke. After I left for my assignment in St. Paul I never heard from him again. I thought he might write to me from St. Luke's, but he never did".

Father Tobin chose his words carefully. What he was about to say would have a significant impact on the sisters, especially Sister Irene?

"I can tell you the reason why, Sister. He never stayed at the orphanage. He is on the run from the law and from me. The people of Whitefield were correct. Wilfred is a demon, a disciple of Satan. He is responsible for many deaths, killings that defy human understanding."

Sister Irene let out a sob and put her hands to her face.

"I'm sorry, but I must ask you some tough questions. I want you to think, on the day Sister Agnes fell, was she left alone?"

"Father, my name is Sister Elizabeth. I was assigned as her caretaker for that day. Because we are so under staffed, Sister Agnes does not receive full time care. She was checked, and her needs attended to, on the average of every twenty to thirty minutes."

"So when she was left alone, some one could have gone up to her room without your knowledge?

"I suppose so, Father, but how would he leave?"

"When you found Sister Agnes at the bottom of the stairs, what was the first thing you did?"

"Why, I ran for help."

Father Tobin stood, placing his coffee cup on one of the end tables.

"That's when he came back down the stairs and left. It had to be Wilfred! Sister Irene, can you give me the directions to the hospital where Mrs. Sorenson is a patient and also the address where I can locate Bishop Kirkpatrick?

"It's not exactly a hospital, Father, more like a prison. Bishop Kirkpatrick is in the communicable disease ward at the city hospital. I'll write the addresses and directions."

"Also, I would like to borrow a car from the parish and I will look in on Sister Agnes before I leave."

With nothing more to discuss, he excused himself and made the climb up the stairs to Sister Agnes's room. Approaching her bedside, he placed her hand in his.

"Sister Agnes's, my name is Father John Tobin. I have been sent from the Vatican to find the boy, Wilfred, and destroy him. I know he is responsible for your pain."

Blessing her, he leaned forward and spoke softly into her ear.

"He chose you to bare the indignities that he endured while nailed to the cross. You have shared his pain and suffering. He rose from the dead, and so shall thee."

Father Tobin felt her hand squeeze against his. Standing back upright, he watched as Sister Agnes's eyes opened and she gave him a glorious smile.

"Because you have suffered his pain, he has cast out the evil from your soul. Let us pray for the miracle he has just blessed you with."

When they had finished, he smiled, turned, and went down the stairs. Sister Irene met him with his directions and the keys the parish cars.

"Thank you, Sister Irene, I shouldn't be gone too long. By the way, you might go up to Sister Agnes's room. She's asking for you."

As Father Tobin drove the car into the parking lot, he read the sign over the front door.

" MINNESOTA STATE ASYLUM"

Walking briskly, he went to the front entrance and rang the bell. The door opened and a middle-aged man wearing a wrinkled gray suit greeted him. Father Tobin knew that he had been spotted walking toward the building, and this would be the facility's administrator.

"Father Tobin. I am from the St. James Parish and I would like to visit one of your patients."

"I am Joel Haywood, the hospital administrator. What is the patient's name?"

"Emily Sorenson."

An expression of surprise came over the administrator's face.

"Father, I'm sorry, but she passed away a few days ago. Her son had visited her, and shortly after that, she was found deceased in her room. It appeared that she either banged her head against the door on purpose, or tripped and fell. The latter made more sense, as her nose was broken. She had a laceration on top of her forehead that resulted in severe blood lost. It was the official cause of death."

"I see Mr. Haywood, and where is she now?"

Father, I pray she is at peace. She was buried across the street in the state cemetery."

Father Tobin was not surprised. Deaths were often poorly documented in these kinds of intuitions. He doubted that the coroner even took the time to look at the body.

"Did her son sign in, Mr. Haywood?"

"Of course, we are mandated by state laws to require visitors to sign the registrar each time they visit. I remembered him, as it was her first visitor. The kid's name was Frankie Sorenson.

Chapter 35

Wilfred found himself wandering about with no plan in mind. He could go by St. James, but who could he harass there? Sister Agnes' bones would not be healing for at least six months. His poor stepmother was in a long term, permanent, sleep mode, and the Reverend Kilpatrick was hospitalized with the itch. He could stop by and see the Monsignor, but with him not knowing who gave him the scab face to begin with, it would not provide much enjoyment. He could tell him, but it would not do much good. By this time, the Reverend probably didn't even have any ears left. They probably kept his hands immobilized just to keep him from scratching his face off. Maybe at another time he would stop in for a visit. Besides, the good bishop was not going anywhere soon.

Wilfred was giving his next move a lot of thought. No matter what ideas popped into his mind, he always came back to the same conclusion. There was only one place to go, and that was back to his old hometown. Nobody in Whitefield would recognize him. He would visit the convent and the old homestead, plus he wanted to pay a call on a Lutheran to thank him for his kind words when the Sorenson's house burned down.

When his business was finished in Whitefield, he could always go up to the Indian reservation. By now, the old Medicine Man must have made his final journey to the big teepee in the sky. Wilfred would never forget what he told Todd and Janice Ingram.

"Take the baby to the center of the lake, weight him down with stones, and cast him into the waters."

Wilfred did not know just when, but the Medicine Man's sons or grandsons had better start learning how to swim with thirty pound rocks strapped to their backs. Hell, maybe he would even look up good old mom and see how she liked being fed to the dogs.

The convent was the most important because it was where he spent the first six or so years of his life. Since his true, demonic identify was unknown to the Sisters, his brain was able to gather and store knowledge that would take years for an average child to absorb. Although his outward appearance was that of a child, he was a very mature individual. The only thorn in his side was being baptized a Catholic, but there were a lot of baptized Catholic's in hell. The more he thought about returning to the old homestead, the more excited he became.

He was wandering around the loading docks of Duluth's largest vegetable and fruit market, when he overheard one of the drivers complaining that he had to go out of his way to make a delivery in Whitefield. Stretching a canvas tarp over his load, the driver tied it down securely and went into the shipping office to get his paper work. It was with relative ease that Wilfred slipped undetected under the canvas tarp and into the back of the truck.

During the trip, the driver stopped for coffee a couple of times, but he never approached the rear of the truck. Hearing increasing traffic and the truck slowing down, Wilfred took a quick peek outside. A sign read, "Welcome to Whitefield."

Entering the center of town, the truck started to slow down in front of the A & P store. For Wilfred, this was a good place to jump ship. Easing carefully off the back of the truck, he dusted himself off, and took a look around. The town square was bustling with people shopping and enjoying the warmth of the day.

He was afraid to ask for directions, thinking it might look suspicious, especially if he happened to ask someone local. None of the street names were familiar. One weathered sign that stood alone had a faded arrow pointing in the direction of a dirt road. The wording was barely legible, "Pine Street Cemetery."

He knew that the convent was on the same road as the cemetery. That was to be his first stop. If it was not in too bad shape, perhaps he could stay there overnight. In fact, he had better move along, as he would not have much time before it got dark. In the morning, he would visit the homestead. He would have to come back into town and take the road behind the courthouse. That, he remembered. Having eaten a lot of fruit while riding in the truck, he was feeling fairly strong.

Twenty minutes later he was standing in front of a shell of a building. Dusk had arrived, but he could see that the convent had been completely ransacked and vandalized. Anything of any value had been removed, including electrical wiring, plumbing fixtures, and even the wood that formed the door casings. The roof was mostly caved in, and what was left appeared to be hanging by a thread. Walking around to the back, the white crosses had all been pulled up and destroyed.

Standing motionless as darkness approached, Wilfred could hear the babies crying. They were of his breed. He had lived; they had died. They were all the paid results of man satisfying a sexual desire. Wilfred was agitated. He had no reason that would justify utilizing his powers. Silently, he implored Satan to intervene. The ground began to shake and the babies stopped crying. The graves opened and the babies rose, one by one, their deep, red eyes glowing with hate. Suspended in air, wrapped in their white sheets, their tiny bodies glowed in the dusk of night.

"Go, my little demons, go into the depths of hell where you will be able to extract your revenge from those who created your very being."

Wilfred watched as the ground opened, flames shot upward with a deafening roar, and the babies descended into the open arms of Lucifer.

Making his way back into the remains of the convent, he felt his way to an open spot on the floor. Making himself comfortable as possible, he lay on his back and slept through the night.

As luck would have it, he awoke at dawn to look into the eyes of a rat sitting on his chest, probably trying to figure out how his nose would taste. He would never get that chance. While the rat continued to ponder Wilfred's nose, Wilfred picked him up by the tail, held him upside down, and bit off its head. Peeling the skin downward, similar to eating a banana, Wilfred finished him off. He could not have asked for a better breakfast.

Chapter 36

Father Tobin was upset over Emily Sorenson's death. He could have asked to see her room but he knew he would be shown a setting constructed specifically for this type of inquiry. He would never see the room she was actually kept in, if indeed it was a room and not a cell. If he insisted, they would show him padded cells, emphasizing that they were only used when a patient became violent. It was for their own protection and the safety of the staff until the patient could regain stability.

This, Father Tobin knew, was all show and tell. Most of the cells would have bare walls, a metal bed, and a hole in the floor used for relieving body waste. If lucky they would be hosed down with cold water once a week.

There was no doubt that Wilfred Magnum had been responsible for Emily Sorenson's death. In her condition, it would not have taken much to drive her over the edge. Father Tobin knew he had missed Wilfred by a couple of days. He was afraid that he might have also gone after Monsignor Kirkpatrick.

At the Duluth General Hospital, he located the Information desk and asked directions to the Communicable Disease Ward. He could not help wondering if the demon had already been there and what he might find.

At the Nursing station he was quick to inquire.

" Is there any record of a young man being here to visit with the bishop?"

When the answer was no, he felt greatly relived.

"My name is Father John Tobin and I have been sent from the Vatican to inquire about the status of the Monsignor Kirkpatrick."

The nurse was polite, but firm. She would call the attending physician. No one, but no one, was ever allowed to visit the bishop. Within a few minutes, the doctor arrived and introduced himself to Father Tobin.

"We are extremely cautious in the handling of the Monsignor. We have not been able to identify the organism that caused his condition. So far, he has not responded to any of our treatments. We cannot allow him a visitor for fear of contamination and that it might be communicable. I am afraid, Father, that his prognosis is very poor."

When the doctor finished, Father Tobin reached into his coat and retrieved a small bottle.

"Doctor, healing is a very complicated mystery within the church and one that I myself cannot explain. The Holy See himself gave me this small vial of solution to have sprinkled over the bishop's body. He will be completely cured. You may hold him as long as you think necessary, to be satisfied that he has been restored to perfect health. What publicity you seek is strictly a decision of the hospital. Notify the Auxiliary Bishop of St. Paul, and he will make arrangements for the bishop to be picked up.

Walking back to the car, Father Tobin felt uncomfortable that he was not allowed to witness his instructions being carried out. He would call in a few days to ensure the bishop's recovery and release.

As Father Tobin turned into the driveway of St. James, he noticed that there seemed to be an overabundance of activity. The lights were all on and the parking area was full. A black limousine was parked in front of the entrance. Father Tobin's first thought was that perhaps the bishop from St. Paul had arrived for a visit, or somehow the celebration was connected to the recovery of Sister Agnes.

Leaving his car, he opened the front door and entered the visiting room. As he approached, everyone there watched for his reaction. Sitting in the corner on a large chair, his red cape draped over his shoulders and wearing his red beanie, sat Cardinal Cassinelli.

Father Tobin was completely surprised. Crossing the room, he knelt on one knee and kissed the Cardinal's ring.

"Your Excellency, what on earth are you doing here?"

Chuckling, the Cardinal motioned for Father Tobin to rise.

" Checking on you!"

The remark produced spontaneous laughter from the sisters.

"No, Father Tobin, it has nothing to do with you. The Holy See called me to his office. He is fast approaching ninety years old, and is not in the best of health."

Motioning for one of the sisters to bring the priest a chair, he continued. Father Tobin and the sisters were listening intently.

"'Within the college of Cardinals there is a strong possibility that I would be in contention to be named the next Pope. Therefore, the Holy See advised me to take a vacation, travel about the world, meet old friends, and do some campaigning. I took his advice and here I am."

Father Tobin shook his head.

"This certainly was a surprise, Cardinal. We are honored that you made time to visit us here at St. James."

"It is my pleasure, Father, but I must be leaving shortly."

The Cardinal took a deep breath and then asked the sisters if they would mind leaving as he had some business to go over with Father Tobin. The sisters quickly and quietly left the room.

"So, Father Tobin, tell me about this Wilfred."

"I am closing in on the boy. In fact, I just came by to tell the sisters I am on my way to the town of Whitefield, I believe that's where he is."

"Excellent, Father. I would like to accompany you, but I am on my way to visit a very old friend at St. Mary's in St. Paul. Besides, I am getting a little old to be chasing after demons."

Father Tobin stood as Cardinal Cassinelli continued to speak.

"Before we part company, I would like you to help me up the stairs, so we could visit and pray for a few moments with Sister Agnes."

"That would be wonderful, Cardinal. I will summon the rest of the

Sisters to join us."

Chapter 37

Taking a last look around, Wilfred had absolutely no feeling for the ruin of the convent. He was sorry that he would not be around when the fourteen empty graves were found. That alone, should spread even more panic among the good folks of Whitefield.

Walking at a steady pace, it took Wilfred little time to reach the outer fringes of the town. Staying away from the public square, he cut across the back lawn of the town hall and onto the road that led to the Sorenson farm. He walked for nearly an hour before he started to recognize some familiar landmarks. He knew that he was getting close. Fallen fence posts, held together by rusty barbed wire, ran along the side the road eventually leading to a wooden mailbox. The paint was faded, but the name "Sorenson" was still legible.

Following the driveway, he entered the yard and went directly to the cellar hole where the house once stood. Half filled with stagnant water and rotted pieces of burnt timber, there was not very much left to see. The stone foundation had begun to fall inward from the constant abuse of the weather. Turning to look across the yard, he could see that the barn was still intact and appeared to be in good repair.

Walking over to it, he opened the side door and stepped inside. It had pretty well been cleaned out. The hay had been removed from the lofts but enough had been left behind for him to make a very comfortable bed. Falling into the hay on his back, Wilfred looked up at the roof. This was a very nice place to rest for a while.

Wilfred had noticed several small holes dug under the barn's foundation, indicating the presence of barn rats. Barn rats were much smaller than the rat he had for breakfast, but they were usually much sweeter. He thought they tasted more like kittens.

Spotting a manure fork, he jumped down from the loft and picked it up. Walking to the far end of the barn, he slid opened the corral door and stepped out into the holding pen. There were still several piles of manure near the back gate. Selecting the one with the most black flies swarming about, Wilfred plunged the dung fork into the pile. Turning over three full fork loads, he was delighted to find an abundance of earthworms as well as hundreds of fly lava and maggots. Kneeling, he gorged himself until his stomach hurt.

Going back inside the barn, he climbed back up into the loft and flopped on the hay. He was quite content and happy to be alone, but that was not why he had come back to Whitefield.

Fred Johnson checked on the Sorenson place about once a week, mostly out of habit and loyalty to his neighbor. Shortly after the fire, he discovered that the water from the Sorenson well tasted much better than from his own. When he checked the property, Fred always brought along a couple of milk cans to fill up and bring back home. The Lutheran community had plans to raise a house where the old one stood and try and get a young Lutheran couple to take over the farm.

As Fred Johnson pulled into the yard he was surprised to see the barn door open and a young blond lad emerge, carrying a coil of rope and a hook. Glancing at Fred Johnson's truck, but paying no particular attention to it, he walked over to the well. Pulling up beside the boy, Fred Johnson rolled down his window.

"What are you doing here? Who said you could take that rope out of the barn."

Paying him no mind, Wilfred tied the hook onto the rope and started lowering it into the well.

"I use to live here. My name is Wilfred Magnum."

"You must be mistaken, son, the Sorenson's use to live here and they had one adopted son, Frankie."

Stepping out of his truck, Fred Johnson went toward the well.

"Now, I asked you nice, boy. I want you to pull that rope back up and take it back to the barn. Then get off this property."

Turning his head, Wilfred looked directly at Fred Johnson.

"Frankie! Who in the hell would want a name like that? Once I got back to the convent, it went back to Wilfred. It was the name that the nuns gave me and I liked it."

Fred Johnson was uneasy. There was no way the baby could have grown to this lad's size since the fire.

"If that's true, boy, what happened to the rest of the family?"

"The last thing I remember is lying out on the front lawn. The flames reduced Sister Sara and Step Daddy Carl to ashes. It was Step Daddy that touched off the blaze. Sara was already dead from the rot. My Step Daddy didn't even look at me. Just laid down on the floor with rotten face and started playing with matches. You know the rest."

"But how did you get out? What about Elena?"

Wilfred turned back to working the rope in the well.

"I think my dear step mother must have carried me outside, then when she started smelling burnt meat coming from the second floor, she went loony and ran for the pasture. I visited her last week at the funny farm. After I left, she cracked her skull wide open on the bars of her cell. The attendants let the rats feed on her brain for the night, then scooped her up in a plastic garbage bag and buried her in a hole across the street."

There was silence, Fred Johnson was at a lost for words. He was afraid and sweating profusely. It was Wilfred that broke the silence.

"Here, give me a hand. Elena wants to say hello."

It was then that Fred knew that the townspeople had been right all along. The baby was a demon and he had to be responsible for the deaths of the Sorenson's and the Town Constables. Frightened more than he had ever been in his life, he looked to the heavens.

"Oh Lord, protect me from evil and keep me safe. Hear my prayer oh Lord."

"Fred, I know for a fact that's not going to help. For some reason, your man seems to have a hearing problem. Now, pay attention. There are a couple of things I am going to require your help with."

Standing his ground, Fred pointed his finger.

"I know who you are! The town office got a telegram from Duluth telling us that a Father

Tobin from Rome was on his way here to find and destroy you."

"Then I guess I had better speed things up a little. Now, let's see, your wife is home cooking. Don't ask! Believe me, I just know. So, any more grief or comments from you and her face will catch on fire. I don't have to tell you how painful that would be. Might improve her looks, but would it be worth it?"

Beside himself and knowing he was in the company of a demon from hell, he began to beg.

"Please! Please don't harm her, I'll do whatever you say."

"Then I suggest you get over here and pull this rope up."

Going to the well, Fred Stevenson took the rope and pulled upward. The skeleton of Elena popped up out of the well.

"Not much left, is there Fred? I want you to prop her up, so when the priest gets here he will feel welcomed. See if you can do anything with her hair, and put one arm up like she's waving. Now you know why the water from the well tasted so good. In fact, you could say you have a little bit of Elena inside you."

Fred Stevenson had all he could do to keep from vomiting. Only a small amount of hair remained on the skull. Taking his fingers he moved it to the back of her head. Lifting her skeletal arm, he supported it against the well rope.

Opening the door to the pickup, Wilfred motioned Fred Stevenson to join him.

"I want you to drive me to the farm of the Lutheran who called me the little Catholic bastard when I was laying on the front lawn. As I remember, his name was Joseph Finn."

Fred Johnson was scared stiff, how could an infant baby remember a name? Taking a right out of the driveway, he drove the mile and a half to the Finn farm.

The farm was huge. A large white house contrasted with two bright red barns. As the entered the drive, three dogs, teeth showing and growling, ran toward the truck. When they got within ten feet, they suddenly stopped short. Tails between their legs, they ran for the open pasture.

"I don't like dogs, Fred. If they get to close, I'll rip their testicles out and eat them, and they know it!

Fred shaking pointed out the window.

"Here comes Mr. Finn. What do you want me to tell him?"

"That some of his cows are on the Sorenson property and they are sick. I'll scoot over and you tell him to get in. If he asks about me, I'm the son of a friend back east, helping out during haying season."

When Joseph Finn heard that some of his cows were sick, he wasted no time getting into the truck. Paying no attention whatsoever to Wilfred, he directed his questions to Fred Stevenson.

"Are they down, Fred, or can they still stand? Once they go down, they are finished."

Before he could say much more, the truck turned and entered the Sorenson's driveway. Joseph Finn's attention went to the well.

"What in heaven's name is that?"

"I'll bet she's lost some weight since the last time you saw her."

Joseph Finn turned and looked at the boy who was speaking to him.

"And who might you be?"

"Mr. Finn, at one time you called me a little Catholic bastard. Why, I don't know. We should all learn to get along with each other. It would make the world a better place."

"I didn't want to get baptized but those nuns just wouldn't let it go. In fact, it lowered my rating from a demon eight to a demon five."

Joe Finn was paying no attention to the boy's rambling's or to the skeleton. He was more concerned about his cattle.

"Where are my sick cows?"

Wilfred went on as if he had heard nothing.

"Luckily, the Catholic doctrine allows for sacraments to be negated. In the near future, I will be going east. There's going to be a Bishop in Boston that will annul anything if the price is right. That alone will qualify me to get my own personalized devil's fork."

"Fred, what is this kid talking about? Is he a looney?"

Sweating like a stuck pig in the middle of July, Fred Johnson did not know what to say. Before he could answer, Wilfred once again spoke up.

"Mr. Finn, I was the baby on the front lawn. You called me a little Catholic bastard and I'm afraid I have never been able to get over it."

"Well kid, I don't know how you grew so fast, but you were a little Catholic bastard then and you're a little Catholic bastard now. Tomorrow you'll still be a little Catholic bastard."

Fred Johnson was terrified that Joe Finn was inciting the boy.

Wilfred turned in his direction.

"Fred, do you go along with what Mr. Finn is saying?"

Sweat beads rolled down from Fred Johnson's forehead, completely covering the front of his face. His hands were shaking and his mouth was so dry that he was struggling to talk.

"Tell you what. I'll let you think about it while I try to convince Mr. Finn that I am really a son of Satan. In the meantime, go in the barn and find a hammer and a couple of spikes or very large nails."

Joseph Finn was not impressed. Smirking, he watched as Wilfred motioned him out of the truck and then looked to the well.

"Elena, would you come over here and take Mr. Finn down to the barn?"

The skeleton pushed itself off the edge of the well and began walking toward Joe Finn.

"What is this Fred? Some kind of joke? How are you making it walk?"

Fred Johnson's answer was to make a dash for the barn. Opening the door, he quickly disappeared inside.

Joseph Finn suddenly felt the clammy hand of the skeleton grab him by the back of the neck and squeeze. The pain was so intense he thought he was going to pass out. He did not have to be told. He started walking toward the barn.

"My dear half sister, you look so charming today. I'll bet you are thrilled to be out of your aquatic playground. Would you mind putting this Lutheran bastard's back up against the building, about twelve inches from the ground?"

Turning her head, she tried to smile, but most of her teeth were missing and the few that remained were rotten.

"Elena, did I tell you I went to see Mommy? She was really surprised to see me. Later, I was informed that she had hit her head on the cell door and cracked it open. Just as well. She was crazier than a bed bug."

Elena snapped her head around pointing her middle finger in an upward motion at Wilfred. She was definitely ticked off. Lifting Joe Finn off his feet, she held his body against the building. At that moment, Fred Johnson stepped out of the barn carrying several spikes and a large hammer.

"Fred, straighten his arm out and nail his hand to the barn."

Trembling, Fred Johnson took a spike, placed it in the center of his friend's hand, and then struck it with the hammer. Screaming in pain, Joe Finn begged his friend to stop, but Wilfred insisted he keep pounding until both hands were secured firmly to the barn wall. Finishing his grizzly task, Fred Johnson stepped away.

Joseph Finn hung suspended by his hands. His eye's bulging outward, mucous running from his nose, and suffering great pain. He still had the strength to look directly at Wilfred.

"Little Catholic bastard!"

Wilfred flew into a rage. A gust of wind came up with such force that it blew Elena back onto the well. Her hair stood straight up and a few of her bones were displaced.

Approaching Joe Finn, Wilfred tugged the front of his shirt away from his belt. A sharp whistle brought a multitude of brown rats scurrying out from beneath the barn.

Wilfred stepped away from Joseph Finn. The rats, following, scampered around his feet in confusion.

"It will take a while Mr. Finn but I think you will enjoy the ingenuity of the barn rat."

As though on cue they began lining up. Their ears pointed straight up as if they were listening to instructions. Then, one after another they ran the few feet forward, leaped upward and tried to take a bite of Joe Finn's shirt.

"What they are doing is first eating away your shirt so they can start munching on your stomach. They won't touch any of your vital organs or major arteries, so you can enjoy their company for at least the next day or so. They will be all kinds of fun once it gets dark."

Fred Johnson stood watching, he was nearing a state of shock.

"Oh, by the way, Fred, your wife's hair did catch on fire and burned a good part of her face. She should really see a doctor. Rolling around on the floor isn't going to help much. You had better go help her."

Running to his truck, Fred Johnson started it up and sped down the driveway. It would take fifteen minutes for him to get back home.

"Well, my Lutheran buddy, I want you to think about this. I was born to a whore in a shantytown, the very shantytown where your wife will soon be working! Your two pretty daughters will go out west. The Chinese are building a railroad tunnel through the mountains. The government supplies them with white women to keep them happy. Once the girls are addicted to the opium, they wouldn't want to come back home anyway."

Looking around, Wilfred decided it was time to leave. By this time, Fred Johnson would be bringing his burnt headed wife into town and spreading the word about the return of the devil child. It would not take long for the townspeople to organize and come out to the Sorenson farm. As though reading his mind the rats began increasing their speed.

"Mr. Finn, I think there might be a Catholic priest coming by. His name is Father Tobin. He's trying to destroy me for reasons I can't quite comprehend. I'm such a nice guy and the nuns loved me."

The rats had eaten their way through Joe Finns skin and blood was oozing down the front of Joe Finns pants. He hung against the barn, a broken man.

" I am going to leave you now so you can be alone, to say your goodbye's to Mr. Luther."

Overhead the blue sky was beginning to get hazy.

"Say, Mr. Finn, do you see the smoke building up? Your two barns are on fire. Most of your animals are trapped inside. The smell is going to make you feel real hungry.

Turning toward the well, he cupped his hands and yelled.

"Nice seeing you, dear sister. Your going to be a big hit on Halloween Night."

Once again she gave Wilfred the digital salute!

Chapter 38

Father Tobin wasted no time driving to Whitefield. After the Cardinal left for St. Paul, one of the Sisters had approached him and said that Sister Agnes wished to speak to him. She had urged him to go to the Pine Street Cemetery in Whitefield. If Wilfred were seeking a place to hide out, it would be at the grave of Sister Sylvia.

The sign was not very conspicuous, but he was able to spot it. Following the direction indicated by the arrow, he was soon speeding along the dirt road leading to the cemetery. Passing the convent, he gave it little notice. A few miles further ahead, he approached the entrance to the graveyard. Turning, he passed under the archway and came to a stop beside a storage shed.

Leaving the car behind, he walked up the small road leading to the main part of the cemetery. He had a feeling that someone else had made the same exact walk before him. It was late in the afternoon and the sun was beginning to settle into the west. Father Tobin removed his sunglasses and let his eyes adjust to the lingering sunlight. As he walked past a corner lot, he looked up in wonder at a very badly mutilated statue of an archangel, sitting on a large block of granite. The name *Brown* was inscribed on the stone base. He thought it very peculiar that someone would erect such a hideous statue, finally concluding that the Brown family must have had an extreme dislike of angels.

Approaching the top of the hill, he heard a voice coming from his left. At the same time, he felt the presence of evil. Near the edge of the woods, he could see what appeared to be a grave with a young boy sitting cross-legged on top of it. He knew it had to be Wilfred. Without turning his head, the boy yelled to him.

"Come on over and join the party!"

Father Tobin left the road and walked across the field toward the grave. As he approached, a figure stepped out of the woods and made his way to the gravesite. Father Tobin was astounded. There before him was Cardinal Cassinelli! Dressed in his red cloak and beanie, he appeared quite distinguished.

"What is the matter, John? Are you surprised to see me? Did you really think I would let you finish this up by yourself?"

Father Tobin moved in closer to the Cardinal and Wilfred.

"Why, yes I am. What are you doing here? Why the red cape, are you going hunting?"

"Does it look like I'm going hunting? Now, Father, you know what I'm doing here! You shouldn't be lying. You know it's a sin."

Wilfred burst out in laughter.

"Did you hear that one, Sister? The Master said a funny?"

Father Tobin heard a voice that seemed to be arising from the grave.

"I heard, I heard. It's not exactly a railroad station down here."

The Cardinal seemed to be getting agitated.

"I want the two of you to butt out! Do you understand?"

Directing his attention to Father Tobin, he gave Wilfred one last look.

"Now we will have our little chit chat. It would be nice to have a little pasta, bread and wine like we did in the old country, but I guess we can't have everything."

Wilfred quickly spoke up.

"Master, I will get it, if you wish?"

Father Tobin was not surprised to hear Wilfred continuing to use the word "master."

"No, Wilfred. The ambiance is not quite right, and if you interrupt me again, you are going to find out what it's like to be a rock."

There was no response from Wilfred. He merely hung his head downward and stared at the ground. A slight chuckle was heard from beneath the ground. If Cardinal Cassinelli heard it, he paid it no heed.

"How long have you known, John?"

Father Tobin was straightforward with his answer.

"I knew from the moment I entered the Vatican and met you.

I have never revealed to anyone that I can sense evil when it is near. The only exception I made was to inform the Pope's confidant."

"So if I have this straight, when you sensed that I was evil, you made it your business to get word to the Pope? That was very clever. I suppose you were told to watch over me and report any evil doings to the confidant."

"That's it in a nut shell, Cassinelli. You don't mind if I leave off the Cardinal part do you?"

"No, not at all, John. In fact I would like to know your intentions. It won't be long before it gets dark, and I have dinner plans."

Reaching into his pocket, Father Tobin withdrew a small bottle of clear liquid.

"My instructions are to destroy you and your boy, Wilfred, and Sister, makes three."

"John, John. Don't you realize you're just a pawn in the overall master plan? There is a reason why you're here. You are being considered for election as the next Pope! Of course, you would be working for me."

Father Tobin was loosening the cap on the bottle.

"I ask you, John, why do you think it was that you were never able to get near the Pope? Because you would have sensed evil, that's why. I ask you, did he personally give you that holy water? What you've got there John is tap water."

Holding the bottle toward the heavens, Father Tobin prayed.

"Holy Father, in your name, I ask that you destroy these creatures of sin. Send them to the fiery pits of hell."

Wilfred was rolling on the ground, laughing so hard he had to hold on to his stomach. Sister Sylvia was yelling up from the grave.

"Oh Master, please let me come up before I pee myself down here!"

The Cardinal could not control his laughter, as the tears ran down his face.

"Oh, what to hell. Come on up."

The ground trembled, the grave opened up, and Sister Sylvia rose to the surface. She was dressed in her tattered habit and smelling of death warmed over. The Cardinal held his nose.

"That's the trouble with you French, you never wash!"

Sister Sylvia was riled.

"Like there was a shower and a douche bowl installed in the casket."

While the three of them were waggling back and forth, Father Tobin quickly unscrewed the cap from the bottle and splashed them with the holy water. Where the water landed, smoke began to arise and their skin appeared to be melting.

Sister Sylvia was beside herself. Screaming, she kept telling the Cardinal they should not have taken the yellow brick road. Wilfred, jumping around in apparent pain, was cursing the girl, Dorothy, and her little dog "TitTit. "

"I told you, Master, that dog was no good. I should have ripped his gonads out when I had the chance."

Father Tobin was completely caught up in the exorcism. Raising his arms toward the heavens, he shouted out in joy.

"Go, you evil ones! Go down into the fury of hell, where you will stay for all eternity."

Cardinal Cassinelli clapped his hands together.

"Okay, cut! Everybody quiet! This has gone on long enough. It's almost dark and I have better things to do with my time, and I don't think that was the dog's name!"

Father Tobin appeared mystified. The smoke had cleared and there was no damage to their bodies. The holy water had not worked!

"Well, John, so much for the holy water gig. I told you it was tap water."

The Cardinal's voice became much more serious. Wilfred elbowed Sister Sylvia. She let out a moan.

"Wilfred, you are really starting to piss me off. For a demon five, you sure aren't showing me much. One more such incident and you will become an acorn, stowed in a tree somewhere under a pile of winter squirrel shit."

Wilfred gave it his best shot!

"I'm going to Boston, I won't be a Catholic much longer, I'll be a number eight demon before you know it. Please! I don't want to be an acorn."

Turning away from Wilfred the Cardinal next directed his attention to Sister Sylvia.

" Sister Sylvia, what am I to do with you? Your a rotted out, one armed, defunct, Benedictine Nun, with a bad ass record."

"Master, please give me my arm back, some meat on my bones, a big set of boobs, and send me to a house of ill repute in Calcutta. I'll get you all kinds of souls, I promise.

Raising his hands once again, the Cardinal shook his head back and forth. A punk kid and a haggled nun, what did he do to deserve this?

"Okay! Okay! But first, we still have a priest to take care of. It's almost dark, so let us move on. John, the reason you never were allowed near the Pope is because you would have sensed evil. I can see that you still don't get it. John, the Pope works for me! All that tap water accomplished was to make more blisters on Bishop Kirkpatrick's face. This afternoon Sister Agnes had a relapse. She is mentally stable; however, for reasons only known to me, she is shrinking in length. So far, it is about one inch per day. When her total length is reduced to twelve inches, her body will stay at that size. The sisters of St. James have plans to rent her out to a circus, so as to help with the winter fuel bill.

You see, John, you are not talking to Cardinal Cassinelli, but to Lucifer himself."

As he spoke, the sky darkened and bolts of lighting crisscrossed the sky as heavy claps of thunder roared through the black clouds above their heads.

Father Tobin watched as the Cardinal transformed himself into a beastly creature of half animal, half human. His ears were enormous, his face was unbelievably ugly and flames erupted outward from his nostrils. Wilfred and Sister Sylvia fell face down onto the ground. Neither had the courage to look up.

As quickly as it happened, the sky cleared, the thunder and lighting stopped, and the grotesque face of Lucifer changed back to that of Cardinal Cassinelli.

" Well, John, do you accept who I am?"

The transformation of Lucifer right in front of him left his mind trying to believe and accept what he had just witnessed. Still trembling in fear, he was having a difficult time to respond.

"Okay, you two, off the ground and make yourself scarce. I want to explain the facts to Father Tobin. We were on to you when you confided in the confidant, who also works for me. We had been watching you for some time, but to be honest, we did not know about your extra sense.

Pausing for a minute, he looked to see if the priest wanted to speak. With no response forthcoming, he continued.

"Demons like Wilfred and Sister Sylvia have a role to play in my society. However, they are limited on how many souls they can provide for the fires of hell. The Pope, on the other hand is in a position to influence and lie to Presidents, Kings, Prime Ministers and other leaders of the world's greatest populations. You can understand that wars bring me more souls than twenty Wilfred's out on the street working twelve hours a day for twenty years. How many Indian's, could Sister Sylvia bang in a week?"

Pausing Lucifer gave Father Tobin time to grasp what he was saying.

"I started sponsoring wars around the time of the Crusades. Caesar was easy, his behavioral examples brought in a record number of sinners. I had extra shifts working during the Napoleonic wars, but that was nothing compared to WWI and WWII. The atomic age will guarantee the future of hell. This is what I am talking to you about, John. There are some goodie, goodie souls that we lose, but the road ahead for hell looks awesome. John Tobin, I really hope that you would consider joining our team. Pledge your loyalty to me and I promise you the Pope's seat. The entire world will be at your beck and call. The monastery in Belgium is a cover for young nuns training in the art of love. Eight of these special sisters are assigned to the Pope at all times. Perhaps you might prefer boys. That can easily be arranged. Whatever your pleasure, I can supply it. All you have to do is start a war or two and then sit back and enjoy the fruits of life. What do you say, John? Going to join us?"

Father Tobin's response was quick.

"If I reject the offer, then what happens?"

"Then, John, your will take Sister Sylvia's place in the casket. It was nice talking to you. If you're planning for the man upstairs to help you out, forget it. I haven't run into him in a couple of centuries."

Lucifer could tell that Father Tobin was in deep thought.

"After your realm as Pope you will spend eternity in hell, where everything is wicked and wonderful. Don't think you will be alone. We have so many priests, that the bad angels can't keep up with them. They have one hell of a time."

Wilfred could not keep from laughing.

"Master, you crack me up."

Lucifer threw his hands into the air.

"Sister Sylvia, is this demon a pain in the ass or what?"

Her answer was to inquire about her breasts!

Lucifer was at his wits end.

Chapter 39

"This is it John Tobin, time to spin the wheel. I want an answer, do you want to be the next Pope?"

"Lucifer your way is evil and will lead to the ruination of mankind. I pick righteousness and good, and to hell with you!"

Lucifer was furious. His disguise as Cardinal Cassinelli was coming apart. His feet were starting to turn back to hoofs.

"If that is your choice, then to the grave you will go. I am really disappointed in you."

Before Lucifer could continue, Father Tobin withdrew a second bottle from his pocket. Removing the cap he sprinkled the contents out over the three demons, they looked at him in amazement.

"What to hell is this about John?"

"I don't believe one word of your lies. I brought two bottles. This is the real holy water, blessed by every Pope since St. Peter. I was well aware that the first bottle was tap water because I filled it myself. Neither the Holy See nor his Confidant is evil. They told me you would lie and try to make me believe. By my playing along with the tap water, believing that it was truly holy water, you let your guard down. Now it's time to play hard ball."

Father Tobin continued to sprinkle the holy water while reciting prayers in Latin.

The two disciples of evil began to scream as fire and smoke began to overcome them.

Sister Sylvia cried out as her body started to melt.

"Where are my breasts? You promised me!"

Wilfred was also yelling at Lucifer.

"I kept telling you about the yellow brick road and what happen to the wicked witch from the west, but would you believe me? Noooooooooo."

Defeated, what was left of Cardinal Cassinelli wrapped himself in his cape.

"Before I leave Wilfred, I am demoting you to a demon one, you will be reassigned to stoking boiler's and you Sister Sylvia, you will be getting your two new breasts, but they will be the size of golf balls!

Suddenly, Father Tobin found himself standing alone in the Pine Street Cemetary. The Sun had set but the new moon rising above the trees provided him with enough light to see. There was no wind and he welcomed the absolute silence.

Standing atop the grave, he gave his thanks to the one above, that he was able to defeat Satan and send his sorry soul back into the depths of hell.

The Cardinal's red cape was badly burned. Lying in the center of the grave was Cassinelli's small red beanie. The tiny cap had always fascinated Father Tobin. As he reached down to retrieve it, a skeletal hand sprang up from the depths of the grave and clenched onto his wrist.

Rapidly twisting his wrist he could not get the hand to release him. As he tried to pull away from the bony manacle, it exerted even more pressure, pulling him slowly downward. Using every bit of strength he could muster against it, he could not prevent being pulled down onto his knees. As the pressure mounted, Father Tobin realized that the hand was going to pull him down into the open grave. Slowly his shoulder and head slipped beneath the surface into the dark hole. The sound of a hideous voice assaulted his eardrums, so loud that it was nearly impossible for him to think.

"Hello Father John, it's Sister Sylvia your new squeeze."

Pushing and clawing at the dirt that was trying to cover him up, he could just barley see a small light glowing from above? If he could only crawl to it, he would be safe. But once again the hand pulled him downward.

"It's going to be just so wonderful sharing my casket with such a handsome priest! My breasts are small but as they say, anything over a mouth full is waste. Now, who's going to be on top?"

The hand ran up his leg and came to a stop.

"Oh Father, I'm going to call you my big John."

Feeling the casket below him, he roughly pushed the hand away and clawed his way upwards as the skin peeled from his hands. Just as he was going to reach the top the hand once more grabbed him and pulled him downward.

"NO, NO, I WON'T GO WITH YOU, LET ME GO, LET ME GO!"

"Father Tobin, Father Tobin. It's okay, it's okay. You are safe."

John Tobin slowly opened his eyes. Looking up, he blinked several times trying to focus his eyes. Slowly, he made out the shapes of fluid bottles and blood plasma units hanging above him. Following the tubing downward, he could not see where they entered into his arm, but he knew they did.

"Don't try to move. You're in an Army Field Hospital. You suffered some very bad wounds. You have been unconscious for the past four days. If you can understand me, blink your eyes."

Blinking his eyes, Father Tobin turned his head slightly toward the nurse. This small amount of movement caused him great pain and for a moment he thought he was going to loose consciousness again. His vision was blurred but he could see that the nurse was wearing a white nurses uniform with a large red cross on its front. Turning his head back, he felt, relief.

"We thought we were going to loose you, Father, but you put up one heck of a battle. You just wouldn't give up. It was as though the fight was between good and evil. You must have won."

A loud explosion was heard nearby, followed by three more.

"They are getting closer, Father. Just about all of the patients have already been moved back behind the lines. The doctor is coming over to see you, he will tell you more."

A blondish looking young man stood looking down at him. It was hard for him to believe doctors could be so young. "I see you have returned back to real world. Your wounds are so severe that it would be impossible to transport you back behind our lines. If we tried, you would surely die from spontaneous hemorrhaging.

The doctor moved closer to Father Tobin's bed.

"The Vatican has used their influence to provide you safe passage through the German lines to their private hospital under St. Peter's Square. We are not far from there, maybe twenty kilometers."

Cardinal Cassinelli, a very powerful Vatican official used his personal friendship with the Fuhrer to arrange for your transportation. He will be in charge of your complete care. Basically he's a nice guy but since he lost his beanie, he has been ugly as hell.

"Your nurse has volunteered to stay with you, I don't know if you have had a chance to talk, but Sister Sylvia is one of our best.

Leaning way down he whispered into the priest's ear.

"Look at her breasts, can you believe it? They're the size of golf balls!"

This was too much for Father Tobin to comprehend. He must be losing his mind.

He tried to move but couldn't. He felt the restraint straps around his arms and legs. Sister Sylvia waited for the Doctor to step back and tend to the intravenous injections. Quickly she ran her hand up the priest's leg. Struggling in pain he turned toward her. She smiled, he gasped. Her teeth were rotted and her face skull like. Yellow slime dripped from her nose and on to her chin.

"You got a way once big John, but not this time!"

Reaching into his surgeon's coat the doctor removed a pair of hemostats and as Father Tobin watched he used them to close off the blood flow from his plasma unit.

"Your going to get a little faint headed but we don't want you getting too well, do we? If you need anything, ask for Wilfred, Doctor Wilfred Magnum! Now if you will excuse me, I got this sudden hankering for a French rat."

"Doctor Wilfred before you go!

"Yes Sister Sylvia?"

"I know he's in a lot of pain, but would you be mad if I defrocked him?"

"You might as well, once the Cardinal's boys have a go at him, you'll have to stand in line."

"Okay Father John, who's going to be on top?"

The inside of Father Tobin's mouth was dry; wetting his lips with his tongue he screamed as loud as he could.

"You win Lucifer! You win! I'll do what ever you say. I'll be the next Pope, just get these creeps away from me."

"Sorry, John, you had your chance. Doctor Wilfred took the offer. Now it's just you and Sister Sylvia."

"Lucifer you won. You have my soul. I have broken my vows. I am an outcast. I have become evil. At least cast me in with the young nuns at the monastery! Why do I get stuck with Sister Sylvia?"

"Because, John, **that's the HELL of it!**

A special thank you to my editor,
Joel Glen Howard.

Glen, as he prefers to be called is the most remarkable man I have ever met. Our friendship dates back many years, when he was the proprietor of his own accounting firm.

Glen has struggled over the past 38 years with ankylosing spondilitis, a disease that gradually causes the moving parts of your skeleton to become fused. He has undergone five joint replacement surgery's, three skin grafts, two hernia repairs, transplanted a piece of his bone from his hip to his spinal column to strengthen a fractured and compressed vertebra, wore a halo traction for five months and endured various other procedures and treatments.

His longest hospital stay was 91 days and his longest stay at a rehabilitation center was 190 days.

While all this was going on Glen managed to find time to get married, buy a home, earn a graduate degree, and start a business that he ran for 21 years.

His wife Betty, a wonderful lady, died after a long battle with a debilitating disease. Shortly after, Glen's legs stopped working. Unable to walk he would require personal care attendants.

Making a decision to sell his business, he moved back to his hometown, Brunswick,

Maine. There he found the pay scale so low that responsible attendants were difficult to hire. He decided to enter a nursing home. To make matters even worse his elbows locked in place, he would have to be fed. Finding the care so sub-standard and unreliable he checked himself out and moved back to his home.

Glen was not one to sit by and let sub-standard health practices be endured by seniors and people with disabilities. He started a one-man campaign to make changes, and changes he made. He started by writing his first article, "A GLIMPSE INTO DEATH'S WAITING ROOM: THE NURSING HOME. ** The article received a great deal of attention. Soon, volunteers were helping him to sponsor a bill for the increase in pay for Health Care Providers. On February 28, 2006, he attended a meeting of the Maine State Legislature, where he gave testimony in behalf of the Health Care Worker and the Disabled. Obtaining the support of Governor John Baldacci (D-ME) legislation was drafted.

In March 2006, article LD 1991was voted on by the Maine legislative body and approved.

He is now hard at work to bring health care to the disabled and to provide medical benefits for the health care provider.

** I urge you to contact Glen at<scarponi75@myway.com> and have him email you his article or a condensation by mail.

Postscript:

After reading my first novel "NEWPORT" Glen was so encouraging that he insisted that he edit my next novel. I am so pleased and thankful for his help. To edit material on a laptop using a pencil placed between your fingers, bed ridden and in constant pain seemed to me to be an over whelming task. His answer! "For a Bowdoin man, it's a walk in the park."

Thank You Glen, your friend
Edward T. Duranty

Printed in the United States
74151LV00001B/73-96

9 781425 996918